The
LAND
where
STORIES
END

David Foster

The
LAND
where
STORIES
END

As narrated by the angel
depicted in
'Madonna con Bambino e due angeli'
by Filippo Lippi

BRANDON

First published in Britain and Ireland in 2003 by
Brandon
an imprint of Mount Eagle Publications
Unit 3 Olympia Trading Estate, Coburg Road, London N22 6TZ, England
and Dingle, Co. Kerry, Ireland

ISBN 0 86322 311 7

Mount Eagle Publications receives support from
the Arts Council/An Chomhairle Ealaíon.

Text by David Foster, with support from the James Joyce Foundation
and the Brisbane *Courier Mail*

Madonna col Bambino e due angeli by Filippo Lippi
from SCALA Group S.p.A., Firenze
Chapter images by Mattheus Merian from *Atalanta fugiens*

Jacket design: id communications
Front cover photograph: Steve MacDonogh
Printed by the Woodprintcraft Group Ltd, Dublin

First published in Australia by Duffy and Snellgrove

You want to hear a story
But you've been watching telly
You watch a lot of telly
On telly every day
And when we turn the lights out
Your mind will soon be dreaming
And dreams are only stories
For those who've lost their way

Why do you need stories?
Everyone needs stories
Adults watch the telly
When children go to bed
And fathers read the papers
And everyone likes movies
And mothers buy the magazines
To see what people said

Still you want a story
You want another story
You haven't heard the story
You need to hear, my friend
All right, I'll tell a story
I'll tell you of a journey
A story of a journey to
The Land where Stories End

Three roads to Heaven

Three roads only

Three roads that take us to

The Land where Stories End

One is bright and sunny

One is dry and dusty

One is dark and stormy

No fourth exists

Amen

And so to our story

I've always liked a story

I don't like bright and sunny ones

I know you hate them too

I don't like boring stories

In dry and dusty language, no

I like them dark and stormy

Is that okay with you?

The King's
BEAUTIFUL
Daughter

A KING HAD A beautiful daughter. She was so beautiful that any man who saw her at once wanted to marry her. Well, the poor old king got so fed up with this he locked his daughter in a round tower where an old monastery had once stood. Round towers have a door about four metres off the ground and this one was no different. If you want to know what a round tower looks like, there are sixty-five left, in part or in ruins, through Ireland, a few in Scotland, one on the Isle of Man.

The king accidentally lost the key to the door. He couldn't find it anywhere although he looked for it day and night for what seemed like centuries. And the door couldn't be opened from the inside, to prevent his daughter getting out without his knowing about it. So the king's daughter, who was a sweet-natured girl as well as very beautiful, sat patiently inside the round tower waiting for someone to open the door. No one had actually seen her in a very long time but every night she would go to the top of the round tower and ring a little hand bell out the window, once, twice, three times. Lots of people could hear it because it was a peaceful kingdom in those days. It was pretty well covered in forest, there were no cars and there was no telly.

In the end the king was forced to proclaim that any man who could open the door would have his daughter's hand in marriage and become heir to the throne. Such was the king's wealth and the reputation of his daughter's beauty that just about every man in the entire kingdom wanted to try. It wasn't long before the keyhole was damaged by people shoving things into it that didn't really belong there and couldn't easily be removed, and the hinges were bent by people pounding against the door, although this did a fat lot of good because the door was at least twenty centimetres thick. In the end, the king was forced to amend his offer to encourage a more sensible approach from his subjects. Anyone could still try, but if you hadn't succeeded after two goes you were led away by one of the king's executioners, all dreadful-looking fellows wearing leather masks with sharp silver studs and poo all over their hands. They would take you to a dungeon, strap you to a wall and do all sorts of terrible things to your body with instruments of torture, before hanging you by your feet from a wheel while crushing all your joints with an axe handle.

This did reduce numbers a bit at first, but so many men were still trying that the executioners were soon worn out and threatening to go on strike. Because the king, you see, was so very rich and the people so very poor, and the princess reputedly so beautiful, and there was a rumour that anyone who married her would live happily ever after.

A poor woodcutter thought he might have a try. The fact he was already married with about seventeen children didn't deter him in the least. His wife, who was his second wife, couldn't for the life of her understand what he would do with her and the children in the unlikely event of his proving successful, and she was naturally concerned that if he were to fail she would have the entire family to support all alone. But, as the woodcutter pointed out, they were so poor they were bound to die anyway, and he thought it would probably be okay. His wife, who loved the woodcutter very much, decided to trust his judgment, even though she was a jealous woman, with good cause, and they both knew it.

They weren't really all that poor. They had a big hut, but with such a large family the woodcutter simply couldn't cut enough wood to support them. So down sat the woodcutter and his wife, at the kitchen table one night when the children had gone to bed, to mull over the problem with a pot or two of beer.

He was a strange fellow, this woodcutter. Well no he wasn't, he was very, very ordinary. A well-meaning fellow, clumsy and stupid, with a fearful temper. He always claimed his first wife couldn't cope with him, but that was just to ease his bad conscience over having left her. His axe had a habit of flying from his hands to inflict serious injuries on innocent passers-by. Well, they weren't all that innocent. In fact the kingdom was a place of rogues and villains. And thieves; you had to watch your property. And liars; no one told the truth about anything, least of all the woodcutter, who was always finding some excuse or other for his bad behaviour. But just because there were so many thieves and liars about, there were saints and wise women too. Provided you knew where to look for them, or rather, provided you knew *how* to look for them.

After they'd been sitting at the table every night for many years, the woodcutter and his current partner – which was how he described his wife when he spoke to any spinster, the rogue – had to admit they had no idea where to look for the key to the door. As the woodcutter himself was always saying to people he met in the woods, if the king himself can't find that key, what hope has anyone else? And no one really wants to be dragged off by some horrible fellow in a studded leather mask with poo all over his hands.

In the end the woodcutter's wife got fed up. 'Look,' she said, 'why don't you go off and see if you can't find someone wiser than we are. Then you could ask them where the key might be. That's probably the best thing to do.'

The woodcutter thought carefully about this suggestion and in the end decided it was a good one. So next morning, after a breakfast of milk, bere bannocks and sausages to keep up his strength, he said goodbye to his family and went off on his own.

It wasn't long before he was in a deep part of the forest he'd never seen before. It was raining hard by this stage and the woodcutter was soaked to the skin, so he thought he might as well sit down to eat his lunch. As a woodcutter he was used to being soaking wet. The rain didn't bother him. And he always looked forward to his lunch, which he'd usually eaten by nine o'clock in the morning, because his wife was an excellent cook, and he always had with his lunch, as well as with his dinner, a bottle of beer or two and sometimes three, but never more than three. The woodcutter had nothing but contempt for people who drank four bottles of beer with a meal.

As the woodcutter reached for the bottles of beer his wife had provided him, and which he always carried with his food in the knapsack tied to the end of the hazel wand over his shoulder, he thought to himself, Heaven knows why, 'No: if I'm to succeed on this journey, I'd better keep my wits about me, what few I have left.' So instead of pulling the lid off the bottle, he threw his head back, opened his mouth, shut his eyes and let the rainwater trickle in.

A leprechaun appeared from behind a tree. They make shoes for fairies, or they're supposed to, and they wear Phrygian caps.

'What are you doing here?' said the leprechaun. 'I hope you don't mean to cut these trees down!'

'Not a bit of it,' said the woodcutter. 'I'm actually off work today. I'm on a journey. I hope to find someone who can tell me how to find the key to the door. You know, the door to the round tower where the king's daughter's been locked up for goodness knows how long?'

'Go to the Land where Stories End,' said the leprechaun, just before he disappeared. Suddenly, as they always do.

'What was that about,' thought the woodcutter. As he spent his days in the forest, he was used to leprechauns. They didn't usually speak. Their ancestors, as everyone knew, had come to the kingdom by flying over the sea, whereas the woodcutter's ancestors had come to the kingdom by boat.

How the woodcutter wished he could fly over the sea by evening! He was deep in a dark part of the forest where the trees grew so thickly he could hardly see where he was going. In fact, he wished he'd brought his axe with him, but he was to see that axe again sooner than he thought.

At last, just as the sun was setting, the woodcutter came to a clearing but there was no grass in the clearing, just dirt. People were there, though. Travellers. A large group was camped in the clearing, clustered around a campfire, and the woodcutter approached them eagerly. Truth to tell, he wasn't very comfortable in the forest without his axe, and though he worked in the woods all day he always went home to his wife and children each night.

'Hey there!' he greeted the travellers, from the edge of the clearing. 'Mind if I sit down by your fire? As you can see I'm sopping wet. I'm certainly glad you're here.'

When he got a bit closer he wasn't quite so glad. What he'd taken for a group of men and women – a fair assumption, because there were children with them – proved to be all women. You had to get very close to see that, though. Some of them looked like the worst kind of cutthroat he'd ever seen. Fierce, angry creatures, with rings through their eyebrows and noses and tattoos of roses and dragons on their arms, along with those interlacing rings he'd seen on ornamental high crosses. And when the woodcutter got close enough to see the expressions on the women's faces, they weren't smiling to see him. On the contrary, they were scowling fiercely.

'What do you want?' said the biggest, ugliest woman, without looking up. She had a shaven head and stank to high heaven. But she was a woman, to her disgust. The woodcutter noticed that kind of thing. Indeed, he was always being roused at by his current wife because of it. 'Not that I care,' continued the woman before he had a chance to respond. 'And what brings you into the woods at night?'

Now she looked at him intently, with the kind of look that from a man would provoke a fight across a bar room. Indeed, a silence fell over the whole group of women as they waited for the woodcutter's response. He saw with alarm that the little children were huddled together in fear and the smallest were sobbing and being comforted by some of the bigger ones. Furthermore, three of the toughest women had quietly triangulated the woodcutter, like a pack of dogs closing in upon their prey. Without him even noticing, they'd taken up positions so he couldn't see all three of them at the same time. He could see two, and he wasn't much worried by two women because, although he was forty-nine years old, seven times seven, he was strong from chopping down trees. But the one you couldn't see was always the one to put the knife in your neck as you were taking out the other two. It was a technique thieves used. The woodcutter had seen them do it on his way to and from work. He began to feel most uncomfortable.

'Well er I'm er just er ... ' Hearing him stammer and stutter, the two women that he could see exchanged a quick glance and moved a step closer.

'I'm a pilgrim,' decided the woodcutter. That was the first thing that came into his head. He'd often seen pilgrims in the forest, off to visit the sacred well. The thieves, who were always hidden in the forest waiting for people to rob and kill, would sometimes leave them alone.

'What kind of pilgrim?' said the woman who was doing all the talking. She must have been the chief of the women.

'I'm looking for someone to tell me where to find the key to the door,' said the woodcutter, 'if you must know.'

'What door is that then?'

'Oh, the door to the round tower. You know, the round tower? Where the king's daughter's locked up?'

There was angry muttering among the women at this, but the chief of the women raised her fattest finger an inch and they all fell silent at once.

'Tell me,' said the chief of the women, calmly now, 'haven't you a wife of your own? A good-looking fellow like you?'

The woodcutter was about to boast how he'd had two wives and God knows how many girlfriends when he realized the position he was in. Whatever he said here, these women would kill him and probably tear him apart. They would be the last people to understand that men are different from women and all the problems that creates. Eternal problems, irreconcilable problems. Problems that take human minds and energies off more important problems.

The woodcutter was sweating now. Sweat was pouring off him. He wished he *was* a pilgrim. He'd seen pilgrims being murdered by robbers once, on his way to work. They'd all died bravely and one had even died smiling. The woodcutter had never forgotten the smile on that dying pilgrim's face.

'But I can't die yet,' thought the woodcutter. 'I'm just not ready for it.' He thought of all the fibs he'd told, he thought of the times he'd roused at his children, for no good reason except that he was cranky with himself and the world.

'Help!' he shouted. 'Christians to the rescue!' But no one there could help him. The little children couldn't help him.

Just then the silence in the clearing was broken by the sound of male voices as a torch-lit procession of ten or twelve men entered the clearing on the opposite side. They were druids, but each wore a Christian cross around his neck and their leader carried a big one of wood as well, which he held out in front of him as he walked. The monks – for this was what they called themselves nowadays – wore long brown dressing gowns with cowls over their heads, except for their leader, who was bare-headed, with his hair long at the back and shaven on top, but only in front of a line, if you drew a line, from ear to ear. He was a tough-looking man with a broken nose and a scar across his face. Seeing the women and the frightened woodcutter, he took in the situation at a glance and moved his men over, to the woodcutter's great relief, towards the women. One of the fiercer women made a half-hearted effort to block his path, but he thrust the cross in her face to indicate that he was already dead, whereupon she fell back sobbing, to pick up her lover's baby and croon to the poor little wretch.

For a moment there was silence. Just the crackling of the flames from the campfire and the hissing of the monks' torches. Then the saint – for that's what he was – the others were scholars but he was a saint – turned to the body of women and said to them precisely what the woodcutter had been wishing he could have thought to say. A sermon was given to the women, beginning, 'Two wives seem too many, while one seems never enough.' A monk wrote down with a quill, on a calf skin, everything that was said.

The woodcutter was grateful for the saint's intercession. The women had settled down now and were arguing among themselves. One of the scholars, who had a bundle of books in his hand, the kind that have drawings of winged lions blowing their own trumpets and dragons biting their own tails, and roses, with plait and knotwork borders like the tattoos on the women's arms, asked the chief of the women if the woodcutter might perhaps spend the night in the clearing, as there were dangerous animals in the woods, provided he kept to himself and wasn't a nuisance. The chief of the women grudgingly agreed, and so the monks went off into the forest again, swinging their torches and singing a song in the strange language they'd invented that none but they could understand. The woodcutter had been rather hoping they might spend the night in the clearing with him, but they didn't seem to be tired. As for the woodcutter, he was exhausted, but he soon forgot the danger he'd been in and even approached one of the prettier women to ask if he might have a sip of the bottle of beer that she was swigging. She threw the bottle at him, so he drank the lot and crawled off to the edge of the clearing to fall asleep. On the way there he found a crucifix one of the monks must have dropped, so he put it in his pocket, in the hope it might fetch a good price at the market.

Next morning, while the women and children were still fast asleep and, in the case of some of the baldy-headed ones, snoring loudly, the woodcutter jumped up and set off in a very good mood. The sun was shining, the ashes from the campfire were smouldering, and while the clearing was littered with empty beer bottles, he wouldn't have to pick them up. That's the beauty of being a pilgrim. The woodcutter set off, without thinking very hard about it, in the direction he'd seen the monks take.

He soon found himself in a delightful meadow. A dark, clean river ran through it, with an endlessly swirling pattern of foam on the surface, from a cascade he could hear roaring not that far upstream. The flowers that he could see were mostly heather, as he noticed when he looked more closely, although there was still a bit of grass here and there. Most meadows were turning into bogs, for it seemed to be raining more and more often, and the trees were no longer there to keep the rain off the ground. That didn't matter, as you could always build another meadow someplace else, which is how woodcutters make a living. There was a black cow grazing in the meadow, on what grass she could find, a black cow with a white blaze. The woodcutter sat back, very relaxed now, under a big oak tree, the kind a woodcutter will leave to stand to provide a bit of shade for stock. This oak tree had a lower branch that extended right across the river, and the water looked so inviting, and the day was so hot, twenty degrees C at least, and the woodcutter so warm, that although he couldn't swim, he stripped off his clothes and immersed himself in the water – all but his freckled arms – by hanging onto the oak branch. When he got out, feeling delightfully cool from the fourteen degree water, he watched for a while the beautiful patterns the foam was making on the surface, listening as he did to the cascade, and the rustling of the leaves in the oak tree, and the cooing of the wood doves in the forest. Feeling the need to dry off, he walked onto the meadow a little way, to where the soft green grass had not yet been replaced by the bristly, prickly heather, and, stacking his clothes beside him, sprawled out naked and fell asleep in the sun.

He woke not recognizing where he was and jumped up to get his bearings. His heart was beating furiously. It was then he noticed a beautiful girl squatting under the oak tree. She was so beautiful and so very young – she couldn't have been as old as his eldest daughter – the woodcutter felt shame that she'd been watching him. He wanted to get dressed. He thought at once of his wife and how jealous she was of young women, then he started to feel indignant. It wasn't his fault the girl was there! The woodcutter didn't want to bend down to pick up his clothes, if it meant taking his eyes off that girl. It was quiet. It was very quiet. The only movement in the whole meadow was the rustling of the oak leaves, the fluttering of the little moths over the heather flowers, and the girl's jaw, as she slowly chewed her beeswax chewing gum.

The woodcutter hardly dared look at that girl. He'd only ever seen one other girl as beautiful as this in his whole life and that was his current partner. And while his wife was still lovely, at seven times seven she was impregnable, while this girl was only two times seven, three at most.

The girl was squatting under the oak tree on her haunches. She was wearing a pair of wedgies and a short dress and her hair was a thick black lustrous mane that fell down almost to her knees. She was thin, though. Strangely thin. The woodcutter could have encircled her bicep between his thumb and right fore-finger. She wasn't the kind of girl the woodcutter would have thought he was attracted to, and they're always the most dangerous kind of girl. Furthermore, she was a girl of his own tribe and his own wives had been girls of some other tribe. The woodcutter thought, as he stood, of what the saint had said to the women. Once, the woodcutter might have sneaked off with a girl like this and done something very dirty, but if his wife had taught him nothing else, she had taught him to behave himself in that respect.

As these thoughts went tumbling through the woodcutter's head, the girl just smiled at him, chewing her gum. She allowed her big dark eyes to stray to his feet and back up to his face. The woodcutter felt a violent pang of regret. His current partner was past childbearing age and he could have more children with this girl. Not that he really wanted more children, mind. He couldn't feed the ones he had. But he did so enjoy doing a dirty thing with a pretty girl.

There is nothing wrong in a man taking a second wife, even a third. It is realistic. Jews do it, or did, and so do Muslims, and they are both People of the Book. Only Christians think it wrong to take a second wife. The joke is, a Christian shouldn't have a wife at all.

The woodcutter never quite realized how he worked it out but his heart was suddenly in his mouth and he felt he was going to faint with terror. The girl was a *witch!* Knowing himself in terrible trouble, the woodcutter turned to run, but the second he did so, the girl became a fierce black griffin and sprang at him, knocking him down. If you don't know what a griffin looks like, think yourself fortunate. He felt her claws rip into his flesh and her teeth tearing at his throat. He tried to scream but no scream would come. He tried to move but he couldn't. She was killing him! He was dying! And then a wyvern sprang in from somewhere, an orange wyvern with black spots, and the two of them tore him limb from limb. They pulled the skin off his flesh and the flesh off his bones. They ate every piece of him. He was finished. He was dying. He was dead.

And the next thing he knew they had gone, and it was very quiet, and the sun was still in the sky and the wood pigeons were still cooing and the cascade tumbling and the woodcutter looked down at his body and it seemed to be all there. It seemed to be all right. He pinched it, to be sure.

He never should have drunk that beer, he decided. It must have been poisoned with something. Shaking his head with relief and laughing at his own stupidity, the woodcutter pulled on his clothes and walked away. By the time he got to the edge of the clearing he was feeling very relaxed. More relaxed, he realized, than he'd felt since he was a little boy. He turned, to look once more at the beautiful clearing, before he moved on.

It wasn't the same clearing as the one he had entered. It looked somehow ... different.

The woodcutter studied the clearing, puzzled, to see what the difference might be. The oak tree was there, the river, the heather, the meadow, the sound of the cascade, the cow ...

Ah! That was the difference. The cow was still grazing but it was a white cow now, not a black one. A white cow with one black ear.

That afternoon, it grew stormy and dark. The wood-cutter trudged on through the forest, starting to feel very tired. He wasn't sure he could go on. When he'd started on this journey he hadn't been all that serious about it. He certainly hadn't been expecting all this trouble. He thought of his poor wife, waiting for him at home with all those children, and he felt sorry he'd ever left her. But then he thought again of the king's daughter and that cheered him up. From what he'd heard, she was a kind-hearted person, nothing like that creature under the tree. If he could just find the key to the door to the round tower, everything might work out. He didn't quite know how, though.

What would he do with all those pearls he meant to inherit from the king? The woodcutter found himself a quiet spot under a tree and soon went to sleep, though it wasn't yet dark.

Sometime that night he was woken by a terrible noise. Three ogres were crashing through the forest towards him, knocking down the trees and creating a tremendous windstorm. The woodcutter curled into a tight ball, hoping they wouldn't find him, but they did. It took them no time at all. They pulled him roughly from his hiding place and one of them sat him on a stump.

'And where might you be going?' asked the ugliest and biggest of the three ogres. He had blood dripping from his mouth and a big thighbone through his nose, and his one fierce eye was in the middle of his head so he wouldn't look lopsided.

The woodcutter, through his chattering teeth, replied that he was a pilgrim.

The ogre burst out laughing at this, and bits of guts, yellow and purple, sprayed all over the woodcutter's face.

'You a pilgrim! That's the best I've heard today. Hear that lads? And how much pain have you caused, pilgrim? Speak the truth, for once in your wicked life.'

The woodcutter immediately thought of all the people he had harmed, accidentally and otherwise. He thought of his wives and how he'd betrayed them, but he couldn't feel too sorry for that, because he was a man, and if he had to tell the truth, he would tell the whole truth, by God. He would have to explain to this ogre how and why he'd looked at other women his whole life long and how his wives and girlfriends had been the beneficiaries. But he wished he hadn't caused pain to his children, which was the inevitable outcome. And he never should have drunk all that beer, and what about the time when he was seven years old he'd cheated someone and denied it when accused? These were the sorts of things the woodcutter needed to get off his chest. So he rattled on and on, gaining voice the whole time, till in the end the ogre could stand no more.

'Oh that's enough,' said the ogre, pulling a sour face, which wasn't hard for him. 'Anyone would think you were the Prince of Sinners. You're nothing of the kind, you arrogant creature.'

And with that the first ogre took the woodcutter off the stump and put him back on the ground.

Now it was the turn of the second ogre, who picked the woodcutter up and sat him back on the stump. This ogre had the head of a bull and the claws of an eagle. His breath was so hot that when he coughed, and he coughed a great deal, it burned the skin off the woodcutter's nose.

'Were you ever unkind to an animal?' inquired the second ogre. He had a necklace on, made of men's heads, all wearing very pained expressions.

The woodcutter had to concede he had killed hundreds of animals, if not thousands. He was a bit of a farmer as well as a bit of a hunter. He ate the livers of animals he killed, even though they always gave him nightmares. Every man in the kingdom had a bit of a farm and the woodcutter, after all, was seven times seven. He was no boy. He'd cut the throats of screaming pigs, he'd rung the necks of barnacle geese. He'd even castrated young bulls, with his teeth.

Would he mention that to the ogre? It might be better not to. But the woodcutter did give a complete account, as full as he could recall, of every chicken he had throttled, every pigeon he had necked, every fish he'd ever caught, every midge he'd ever crushed, until the second ogre grew just as fed up as the first had been. For as before, the woodcutter grew more self-righteous as he went on. What were people supposed to eat? If you didn't wring the necks of the pigeon squabs they overran the farm.

'Oh give up,' said the second ogre eventually. 'I can't be here all night. There's other villains in this world beside you.'

And with that the second ogre took the woodcutter off the stump and put him back on the ground.

The woodcutter was wondering what the third ogre might have to say but the third ogre had gone to sleep. The others threw a lightning bolt at him to make him get up. He looked a bit like a gum tree, big streamers of candlebark hanging off his body. Staggering to his feet, he grabbed the woodcutter with his horrible dry twiggy fingers and then, with the woodcutter's own axe, which had magically appeared, pinned the woodcutter by his hair to the stump, so he couldn't get up without scalping himself. Then all three ogres went off to have a cup of salted blood from the thermos of blood that ogres generally carry because they have to work such long hours. The woodcutter could hear them discussing his case, deciding the best punishment for him.

'I say leave him where he is,' said the second ogre. 'He can't move and the torcs will rip up his guts and the crores can peck out his eyes.'

'I'd rather get in touch with all the poor tramps in this world, trudging around, whom he could have shown a bit of kindness to, even if it were only a smile,' said the first ogre. 'Let him drown in his own tears.'

'I'm all for setting fire to that stump,' said the third ogre.

'That's all you can ever think of,' said the first ogre. 'You've no imagination.'

'As we can't agree,' said the second ogre, 'let's just nail him to a cross. It's simple, it's effective, and I've a pocketful of snoods and doovers here somewhere, just a mo ... '

As the second ogre went rummaging through his hide with the eagle claw that could drive in a nail no worries, looking for a snood or doover, the woodcutter suddenly remembered the little crucifix he'd put in his pocket. He hoped it was still there. It might be worth a try to pull it out, provided he could find it. It had worked on the women.

Yes! Thank goodness! It was still there, and the minute the woodcutter's fingers touched it, the ogres stubbed out their torches – on the woodcutter's head but he wasn't complaining – rinsed out their cups in the rain and, swinging the woodcutter's axe, stormed off to find another victim.

The woodcutter thought it might be a good idea to put the crucifix around his neck. It might be a good idea, too, not to hurt people anymore and not to be unkind to animals and maybe not to chop trees down, though he wasn't too sure about that. It was his living, after all, and a man had to have a living, didn't he? Then the woodcutter fell into a deep sleep and, as he slept, an angel came down and kissed him, very sweetly and gently, on his face.

In the morning the woodcutter woke refreshed but

still not quite knowing where he was going or what he was doing or who he was anymore. He set off again, with the crucifix around his neck as a breastplate, to keep the women and the ogres away, and he thought he could see a faint path ahead. So he followed the path. It wasn't easy to follow and he often lost it, but he'd thrown away all his bottles of beer, knowing it was important to remain alert. If he lost the track he just went back and retraced his steps until he found it again. That night he slept quietly. He was a bit disappointed when the angel didn't come down and kiss him again, but there you go.

About the middle of the next day, by which time he was getting very, very hungry, and by which time the track had become so easy to follow he felt free to take his eyes off it and enjoy the beauties of the forest, the woodcutter suddenly came upon the sea. Before him was a village of wooden huts. There was a big stone abbey by the harbour, which had a sandy beach, with some upturned boats pulled high on the shore. They were currachs, long thin boats like canoes but made of the hide of a bullock.

The woodcutter was so pleased to be out of that forest and back in a village of some sort he ran excitedly towards it, anxious to grab the first person he encountered to tell them what he'd been through. Such adventure! How he'd been eaten by a wyvern and a griffin, how he'd fooled the terrible ogres and ...

And suddenly he stopped running as a terrible

thought occurred to him. He suddenly recalled that madman, who'd come running out of the forest at home, screaming and laughing at how he'd been eaten by a dragon and a basilisk, and of how he'd killed them both with a sword he found in a stone, and of the beautiful maiden he had saved, and both the woodcutter and his wife had signed a petition asking that the man be locked up and the key thrown away, for his own welfare and the peace of the community.

The heart went out of the woodcutter completely. He just slumped down on the ground. No one would understand him. No one would believe him. He grabbed his crucifix and burst into tears, pleading for the angel to kiss him again.

Just then he noticed an old man sitting on the ground nearby and staring out to sea. When the woodcutter stopped sniffling and looked up to see what the man was staring at, he noticed two rocky little islands that looked like churches with steep double roofs. They were about twelve kilometres offshore. The larger one looked to be green and the smaller one looked to be white. You might ask how the woodcutter could tell what colour they were at that great distance, but people had better eyesight then because they didn't watch any telly.

'What's the name of those islands?' the woodcutter asked the old man politely.

The old man said nothing.

'I feel I'd like to visit one,' said the woodcutter, trying to draw the man out.

The old man looked up with the eyes of a gannet. 'Why?' he inquired.

'I don't know,' said the woodcutter.

This was not the answer the old man had sought. The woodcutter, who had been through so much excitement he had almost forgotten the reason he set out from home in the first place, began to tell the old man his life story, beginning with his earliest recollections. This took all that day, all that night, and half the next day. The old man just listened quietly. He couldn't have got a word in had he tried.

'And why would you want to marry the girl in the tower when you've already had two wives?' inquired the old man when the woodcutter finally ran out of breath.

'I don't know,' said the woodcutter. 'I just think it might work out.'

'And what will you do with the king's pearls? Do you really need all those pearls?'

'No, I don't really want to marry the girl and I don't really need all those pearls,' said the woodcutter. He'd probably keep a few of them, he thought.

'Then what *do* you want?' inquired the old man.

The woodcutter was surprised by his own reply.

'I want to live happily ever after!' he sobbed, bursting into tears.

The old man smiled. Standing up, he pointed at the larger of the two islands and said, 'That is the Land where Stories End.'

Then he disappeared, because he too was an angel.

Without a moment's hesitation the woodcutter ran down to the harbour to find a boatman to take him over. You can guess he wasn't a storyteller.

He did find a boatman prepared to transport him but the woodcutter had to row too. It was a dangerous journey, warned the boatman, and the truth of this became apparent when they got out of the harbour and onto the open sea. A big swell was rolling in because this was the Edge of the World. At times it seemed the boat, which was only a flimsy currach made of cattle hide, would be swamped, but the islands could periodically be seen, so beautiful, over the crests of the swell, and they got bigger and bigger, and closer and closer, till the woodcutter could tell that both were the tops of mountains sticking up out of the sea, and the small one was white because it was a gannetry, all covered with nesting gannets, while the larger, which was not so very far from the smaller, was green because, while it was steep, what soil there was on it was fertile. A few hardy goats and sheep were scrambling up and down the steep slopes.

As the boatman struggled to find a ledge of rock to land the boat upon – there was no beach and no harbour – the woodcutter looked up and there, on the top of the smaller of the two peaks on the green island, he saw an amazing sight. There appeared to be a small village there, with six beehive huts and an oratory, and a steep stairway cut out of the sandstone, two hundred metres up the cliff face. The woodcutter felt he was dreaming. This had to be a dream. The air was teeming with seabirds of every kind: puffins, gannets, guillemots, fulmars.

The boatman thought it too dangerous to try to land as the water was full and a big swell was breaking against the cliff face. So they rowed back towards shore till it got dark and they sat on the sea in the little currach during the hours of darkness, six in all, and continued rowing when it got light.

During the night the boatman told the woodcutter about the village. It was no dream but a hermitage, a 'desert' hermitage, built by some monks who liked to test the limits of human endurance. In winter the gales whipped up seas that broke right over the top of their village, two hundred metres up, drenching it with spray. The monks had to crawl around, sometimes slither. They were forever being blown to their deaths off the cliffs, where they had to go fowling, and drowning, as waves capsized the currachs they used for transport to the mainland. Nonetheless, over the centuries they'd managed to find replacement monks and build a village and carve a stairway up to it, as an inspiration to future generations and a lesson to the fairy folk who had been there when they first arrived. Countless monks had perished in the process, making this beautiful island the site of their resurrection, but others had always come out to take their places, until recently.

Now it was widely believed on the mainland that

only one monk remained.

'They've had to move,' said the boatman. 'This bad weather has beaten them. They was told to join the abbey. Them's the lads in town.'

'What about the one who is still up there?' inquired the woodcutter.

'Won't do as he's told,' said the boatman. 'No one has seen him in a very long time now. He's likely dead.'

Next morning, leaving the boatman sound asleep in his boat, the woodcutter, who couldn't sleep, wandered around the village. A newly married couple was emerging from the abbey chapel, of all places. The boatman, who felt very much like getting drunk, had hoped to go to the reception but he was too tired.

The woodcutter tried to rouse people in the huts but they were all at the reception. He could hear them screaming and yelling. He wanted to ask about the islands but he found the people not keen to talk to strangers. A plague was spreading across the world, caused by people doing dirty things with each other.

Finally, in the very last hut in the village, the woodcutter found an old woman who was pretty deaf and so didn't know there was a wedding reception on. She hadn't heard about the plague either but it wasn't going to bother her.

With difficulty, the woodcutter tried to explain his quest through shouting and hand signals. After listening and watching, puzzled, for hours, the old woman stood up and motioned for the woodcutter to step over the pig, and sidestep the calf, and look at the shrine she had on the wall, which featured a sketch of her patron saint, who was also the man who had founded the island hermitage. The woodcutter thought he looked a bit like the saint who had saved him from the women, but it wasn't a very good sketch.

Next day was fine and calm. The woodcutter and the boatman went back out on the sea in the currach. By this stage the boatman owned, as the fare, the woodcutter's hut and all his possessions, including his wife's walrus and boar tusk pendants. No sooner had they reached the big island – which wasn't much bigger than a football pitch, by the way, but a whole lot steeper – than the woodcutter leapt ashore and started galloping up the hundreds of steps. He couldn't wait to get to the top but, even so, the view was so brilliant, he had to stop at one point to admire it and get his breath back at the same time.

Ring! He heard the tinkle of a little hand bell.

'Why do I feel I have been here before?' thought the woodcutter smiling to himself.

There wasn't a cloud in the sky. How sweet that air tasted! There wasn't a ripple on the sea. The seabirds and the gannets especially were wheeling and diving, filling the sky with colour and movement. The woodcutter shouted, hoping to gain someone's attention, but all the attention he gained was that of the boatman, who was sitting down in his currach.

'Hurry up,' shouted the boatman.

The woodcutter looked through the huts a second time. There was no one on the island.

Ring! The woodcutter heard the hand bell ring again.

'How *could* I have been here before?' he thought. 'Why, that's not possible.'

'Come on,' shouted the boatman. 'Hurry up up there! Oi'm havin a drink with the lads tonight and do you not feel a storm comin? We don't get days like this anymore.'

Just then the woodcutter noticed, as he cast his eyes around, a stone hut he hadn't seen before. It was away from the main village, right up on the very highest peak on the whole of the green island. There was no staircase to it, as far as he could tell, so he ran over and started climbing up the sheer rock face. He wasn't a bad climber because woodcutters are forever climbing trees on the job.

When the woodcutter got to the hut he had to crawl in through a low, small opening. The wind was usually so strong here you never got off your knees.

Once inside, the woodcutter's eyes took a while to adjust to the darkness. He saw what he thought was a ghost but then a shaft of light came suddenly through a hole in the sandstone wall and the woodcutter saw a man's face and the man was holding out his hand and in the man's hand was a key.

Ring! The woodcutter heard the little hand bell ring a third time.

It was the woodcutter's face. It was the woodcutter's own face.

Now that's not the end of our story but you can't tell stories in the Land where Stories End. There are no stories in the Land where Stories End. The main thing to remember is, when the woodcutter set off on his journey he was a young man, but when he took the key from his own hand he became an old one. He should have remained an old man too, but he didn't. He couldn't, with a wife and seventeen children.

Remember the prophet Moses who caught a glimpse of the Promised Land? The woodcutter has caught a glimpse of the Land where Stories End.

He was still a bit worried about the king's daughter back there in the round tower. What would his jealous wife say when he opened the door to release the girl? When he opened the door with his key, though, everyone cheered, and the king's daughter, who was just as lovely as everyone had hoped and expected, laughed with relief. The woodcutter laughed with relief too, and so did the woodcutter's wife, and so did the whole world, and the church bells rang by themselves and a wood dove cooed. Because it was obvious you couldn't do anything dirty with a girl who laughed like that! And so they all lived happily, but not forever after.

Only for a while. Only for a bit.

The woodcutter lost the key to the door about the time the king's daughter lost her beautiful laugh. And the king didn't warm to the woodcutter and wouldn't announce a date for the wedding and wouldn't hand over the kingdom.

One morning the king invited the woodcutter over. The woodcutter, who had never before been invited to the royal palace, at once put on his best plaid and hastened off to meet the king. But the king, wearing a dirty old cloak, was waiting for the woodcutter outside the gate.

'I hear you're thinking of doing a dirty thing with that daughter of mine,' said the king. 'So now you've three wives, Israel, and I no prospect of an heir. Where's the key to that door? I might put my daughter back in the round tower for a spell.'

The woodcutter had to confess he had lost the key to the door. It wasn't his fault, though, as he went on to explain.

The king, having himself lost the key, was obliged to be civil. 'Return to the rock in the sea,' he said, 'and fetch the key again, Israel!' The king always called the woodcutter 'Israel'.

Without hesitation the woodcutter ran off, hoping to create a good impression on the king, who searched for the key himself, night and day, to no avail. Yet though the woodcutter searched the coast of that kingdom, no trace of the island did he find. Oh, he found the abbey, but the abbey was ruined and deserted, likewise the nearby village. Of all the huts that had been there on his previous visit only one remained. Yes, only that deaf old woman's hut was left and she was deafer than before.

'Praise be I found you,' shouted the woodcutter, wanting to hug her, though in the end he didn't as he felt he had trouble enough with women. 'I was starting to imagine I had made the whole thing up. There's a green island off the coast here, dear. Would you know what happened to it?'

'That's a Fairyland,' came the reply, 'so the question is, what's happened to *you*, my lad?'

It was then the woodcutter realized that, like the Apostle Paul, he had lost his way between the Promised Land and the Land where Stories End.

The King's
HORRIBLE
Prison

FOR A TIME the woodcutter sat on a bank of yellow iris, pulling at his grey-flecked beard. He watched an eider duck leading her five ducklings through spindrift on the rocks, which, by the sea, were covered in weed, so that they looked like cows. He listened to the seapies, or oystercatchers, the red bills of which his mother always used for shawl pins, many of them standing on the one leg. Their call reminded him of the sound of his own axe being sharpened. How he wished he could have worked out where that Fairyland had gone! But he couldn't fathom it, as he was never much of a thinker.

If he turned his head he saw behind him the ruins of the abbey, which seemed now smaller than he recalled. A brown ram, with a scrotum the size of a haggis, was grazing the eyebright, a multicoloured flower that grows on the top of any wall on the machair. Where had those wooden huts gone? No trace of them remained. There were not even those violet nettles, where residents do wees and poos. At least the boatman couldn't now claim the woodcutter's hut and his wife's jewellery, and this was just as well as she hadn't been keen to hand it over. Even the old woman's hut, with the shrine of the saint on the wall, was a wreck, and the woodcutter couldn't get another word from her no matter how loudly he shouted.

All that remained of the little village on the Edge of the World was a bit of stone walling – which could have been the ruins of anything really, because the Promised Land was full of ruins, then as now – a wooden hut, all but unroofed and half collapsed, a few broken stone lamps that smelled strongly of fulmar oil and a monumental woodheap of grey oak wood. This stretched as far as the woodcutter could see.

What a heap of oak wood! But no Land where Stories End. This so depressed the woodcutter he said some dirty words. Then he stood up and, brushing the sand from his bum, as he didn't like to crush a good plaid, took the crucifix from his sporran, which was a bumbag he often wore in case he came upon some pearls, and held it before his eyes as it started to rain for the second time in an hour.

The crucifix was moulded pewter with a length of fishing line threaded through. And to think he had worn it around his neck as though he were some kind of saint! Thank the Lord his wife had had the sense to demand that he remove it. A crucifix annoyed her – she was a woman who hated monks – but the woodcutter couldn't bring himself to throw it away completely, and kept it, hidden under a stone quern he used to grind up corn, which was really a job one or other of his many children should have done, only they were all too fat and lazy to do any work of any kind.

The rain was coming down hard now, making stains all along the stone wall. Thought the woodcutter, 'I'll have to go back and tell the king I can't find the key. I don't imagine he'll be pleased but he doesn't much like me. Why, never once has he given me even the one black pearl! My brothers ask when I'm to marry that daughter of his, but I suspect the king's a snob who doesn't think I'm good enough for her. He doesn't want to proceed with our wedding but daren't go back on his word, being king.'

Can you suppose the woodcutter never thought of the king's executioners? When the Land where Stories End disappears, a man walks again in mortal fear.

It was summer in the forest, although so dark and stormy you could see your breath. The woodcutter thought again of that pile of firewood, which made his brow knit. He guessed it had been cut by monks from the abbey or maybe the village men. As fishermen they may have procured it before they'd gone to sea a final time. They had obviously met with some disaster. Oh well, it wouldn't be needed now and as it was just a matter of time before the sea raiders spied it – there was maritime traffic aplenty off this shore of the Edge of the World, the woodcutter had actually seen a sail as he sat on the iris bank – he knew he needed to act promptly if he wanted the heap for himself.

'If I could get that woodheap back to my clachan,' he thought, 'I wouldn't need to fall a green or living tree for years. That would allow me time to mend my stone head dyke, thus preventing my sheep and cattle forever getting out. It's a shame my sons are as fat and lazy as my daughters, because if they were as fit and willing to work as their mother, my current partner, I could ask them to shift the wood for me. As things stand, I shall have to do it myself.'

The rain grew steadily heavier. Soon it was bucketing down, to the point the leaves on the oaks could offer no shelter. As a traveler on the dark and stormy road, the woodcutter was used to being wet, but he had a fresh cut on one foot, which he wanted to keep clean. A cut on the foot is a dirty thing and the woodcutter knew that a man could catch the plague from such a cut.

The trees in this part of the kingdom were oak with a bit of holly and arbutus. The oaks were big trees, centuries old, all swathed in green filmy ferns. Back at the woodheap, grey as herring, there had been a circular slab that had evidently been cut from the very base of a large oak tree. The woodcutter always counted the rings on the face of any such slab and he'd seen from the expert cut that he was not the world's best wood-cutter. This so aggrieved him, he dragged the slab to the Edge of the World and kicked it off. Three times it washed back up but four times he pushed it out to sea until, eventually, it disappeared from his view around the point.

As shadows lengthened the woodcutter sat down to see what he had left to eat. There was no food in his knapsack, though, just four bottles of beer. Having downed the beer and thrown away all the bottles as far as he could throw, he wondered if it was a good idea to walk a bit further on before dark, even though he hadn't the slightest notion as to where he was. Thus, he found himself a bit later dragging himself through the darkening woods, belching and feeling, as mostly he did when drunk, sorry for himself.

He woke the next morning with a dry mouth and a white tongue and a splitting headache and his plaid soaking wet. The first thing he did was to examine his foot, to ensure the cut hadn't opened. It had. He was sitting, head bent, scrutinizing his filthy right sole with his filthy right foot tucked over his filthy left knee, when he heard the familiar squeak of a cow pulling with her teeth on some damp grass.

The woodcutter saw he had fallen asleep the night before on the very edge of a meadow. A dark, clean river ran through the meadow, with an endlessly swirling pattern of foam on the surface, from a cascade he could hear roaring not that far upstream. The cow, grazing in the clearing on what grass she could find, was black with a white sock. The woodcutter felt he had seen her before, in which case the clearing should have had, in a central position, a tree.

'Was it me cleared this clearing?' he thought. 'Wouldn't I leave a tree? Do I not always leave the biggest tree to provide a bit of shade for stock? Oh well, there's no tree here I can see, I must be imagining it.'

He stood up, slowly, with his head sore and the cut on his foot reopened, and the cow looked on with concern. She lowed, with the soft low a cow gives when she has just calved, then turned towards the river, which made the woodcutter suspect her calf was hidden there. The thought of some fresh milk for breakfast appealed to the parched woodcutter's throat, but before he could grab her the cow waddled off with a bag so full she could barely move, and smeared still with the blood and gore from the afterbirth she had just lapped up.

'I'd like to know you better,' said the woodcutter. 'My god, you're a gorgeous girl. How would you like to come home with me?' He knew if he picked up her calf and carried it off, the cow would follow. And while he didn't know where he was, he wasn't bothered by that, for he knew if he just kept moving he'd find somewhere he recognized. It was only a small kingdom.

'Where have you hidden your calf?' he demanded. 'Why, there's milk dripping from under you. My god, you're a beautiful girl! I wonder what I should call you?'

The cow belonged to the king. A meadow without a fence, as the woodcutter knew, was the king's property. Nonetheless, a man who found a cow in the woods would take her home.

The woodcutter thought he might fence the meadow and give it to some lazy wretch of a son, and was actually starting to pace it out, when the cow stood stock still and arched her back to do a wees.

It was then the woodcutter noticed a girl, squatting on the oak stump. As soon as he set eyes on her he realized where he was. He had stumbled again on the meadow in which he had had that bad experience, and here again was the beautiful witch who had torn him limb from limb.

She smiled and patted the stump. You may be certain the woodcutter made sure he touched his crucifix, but he pulled in his belly and straightened his plaid as he sat on the stump as bidden. The cow, meantime, finished her wees and wandered off to feed the calf.

'Well,' said the beautiful witch, uncrossing her legs, 'have we met before?'

'In this world or that,' said the woodcutter. 'You had the measure of me, though. You turned into a fierce griffin who tore me limb from limb!'

'I don't do that sort of thing now,' smiled the witch. 'I've given that kind of thing up. My one desire is to cure the king, the poor sick man. Before we speak,

I must caution you I never leave my clearing, so all you say must relate to what I have seen. I never saw a town.'

'Nor me,' said the woodcutter, 'and I doubt such a place could exist, for what would they do with all their wees and poos?'

'You'd like to do a dirty thing with me,' observed the witch.

He opened his mouth to respond but the words seemed not to want to come out. She had put him under a spell.

'I never care if I see again any man with whom I do a dirty thing, and furthermore, I will do a dirty thing with any man at all who happens by. Do you want to compete with those who went before you? No one need know.'

Made ardent by the invitation but also a bit disconcerted, the woodcutter hastened to tell the girl about his two wives. The first had been no more than a child. As a young man, he explained to the witch, he'd been an idle, drunken lout. Tears flowed, as he spoke of how he'd mistreated his first wife. He was keen to go on and explain how he'd met his second wife, which he enjoyed speaking of, but the witch interrupted him, insisting he recount what in his view constituted bad treatment.

So he spoke of late nights, drunken revels, wood squandered, duty neglected. These were matters he mentioned but seldom. He didn't really understand why the witch needed to know, although she seemed sympathetic. When he mentioned a cellar maid, she interrupted again.

'You don't regret your girlfriend so don't pretend you do.'

'Part of me regrets her and part of me does not. But in the Land where Stories End a man abhors all women.'

'You don't live in the Land where Stories End. We all live in our bodies! I tell you this: if there were such a thing as True Marriage in the Promised Land, the children that are born to it could do no dirty thing, as they would have no need or wish to do a dirty thing. The instant we forgive our parents is the instant desire departs.'

'Hold on a minute,' said the woodcutter, though he suspected there was truth in this; 'How is our human race to persist if no one ever does a dirty thing?'

She wouldn't answer this. After a bit of hesitation, he left the clearing. He'd soon forgotten everything the witch had said to him.

As he had neither food nor drink he was hungry and weary by the time he got home, but if he had in mind a feed of milk and honey, with a sleep to follow, his wife soon put him straight.

'There's a swarm of bees behind the head dyke,' she announced as he staggered into his hut. 'You'd better get straight onto it. I wouldn't like to see a neighbour take that swarm. We're almost out of honey.'

Grumbling as how he was one of the few men he

knew who kept a hive, the woodcutter searched his hut for a straw skep in which to house the swarm.

'Don't your neighbours love your honey,' said his wife, encouragingly. 'And don't your children love it.'

'Speaking of children, where are they? It would be a boon, were a child to help create and direct the smoke.'

'I won't have a boy of mine stung. Besides, they all went to the booley.'

'What! They went up to the booley?'

'They all went up to the booley.'

'But I thought we agreed a few was to sharpen the noses on the sheep so they could eat between the rocks. My god, we don't need seventeen children to tend the stock on the booley.'

'Don't you be talking like that! Those that remained were pining for their siblings, oh it was a piteous sight. I told them to take the rest of the furnishings and what was left of the honey and the corn and not to let me see them again before the Feast of Samhain.'

'So there's no honey?'

'There's no honey and no milk. But if you want to do a dirty thing, the coast is clear. We're all alone.'

She winked. Cursing, the woodcutter, who'd been so looking forward to a meal and a sleep, limped off, with the skep in his hands and some wool, to hive the errant swarm. His wife didn't like to see a man, unless the fruit of her own womb, idle, and even the smallest swarm, as she knew, have their bellies full of honey. If the woodcutter could secure a bellyful of honey from each bee in the swarm, that would compensate him for the pain of the stings he was certain to receive.

The woodcutter lived with his wife and children on a few acres in the uplands of the kingdom on a hill of pinkish gneiss swept bare by driving winds and pouring rain. There had been pines here once, under the blanket bog. The clachan infield, which the woodcutter shared with a dozen neighbours all bearing his own surname, extended from a loch which looked like a burn, yet by which hooded crows fought herring gulls. The woodcutter thought ruefully, as he surveyed his own poor pasture, of the machair by the woodheap he'd found on the World's Edge. Growing behind the marram grass that grew in the white dunes it had been a brilliant sight, even in rain, with white flowering hogweed, blue hairy tare and yellow bedstraw among the corn poppies. A bee brave enough to fly through rain to the machair would find a feast of nectar, whereas up here all they had to suck on was heather, which often as not they couldn't or wouldn't work. The cattle did well, for milk and honey are like male and female; good in combination, though what suits one won't always suit the other.

The woodcutter kept his own bees in the forest, hidden from honey thieves, and he didn't like heather honey. His few rotten teeth found it too problematical.

A straw skep in one big hand, a smouldering lump

of greasy wool in the other, the woodcutter went to the infield to check his main corn crop before hiving the swarm. The corn he grew was bere, an ancient barley with four rows of spikelets. He climbed the earth bank and beyond it the stone wall delimiting his infield from his out. On the outfield the land climbed steeply to a treeless summit wreathed in cloud, and the woodcutter saw that his wooden hurdles, which he'd ordered stacked away, were out, and for no reason as the black cattle they were meant to enfold had long since decamped.

A pair of young, bored mischievous steers had broken out to join the wild cattle and their mothers had followed. There would be no poos with which to fertilize next year's outfield corn.

The cattle had gone into the oak forest that still covered most of the kingdom, a forest so dense you could swing, it was said, through the crowns of the trees from sea to sea. The loss of the cattle was due to the woodcutter's head dyke being in a state of disrepair, but luckily, most of his cattle were at the booley with his children.

As he hived the swarm the woodcutter never thought of the king's daughter. He thought again of that pert cellar maid with whom he'd once done a dirty thing. He often thought of her. And he thought of his current partner whom he loved so very dearly, but mostly he thought of the witch with whom he'd spent the morning in the clearing. She'd certainly had two lovely arms and oh what beautiful legs, but she was a feminine person? No. She was far too overbearing.

The woodcutter enjoyed the dirty thing he did with his wife, and when it was over, he cleared his throat and began to tell her of the woodheap he had found. She wasn't keen to listen and threw a whalebone pot at his head, which missed. Puzzled by his wife's behaviour, the woodcutter went outside to feed his hounds, the dozen or more who were begging him to be fed.

These hounds, far too fat and lazy to hunt a fox let alone a wolf, spent their time lying by the fire in the hut when not scratching fleas from their coats. They wouldn't dream of going to the bothy on the booley or guarding an outfield, and indeed, the only time they came to life was when, as now, they were due to be fed, or if some stranger happened by the hut, whereupon they would all run out and mill round, wagging their tails. Feeding the hounds was meant to be a duty of the children, which to their credit they performed, but since the children were rarely home in summer and the hounds wouldn't leave the hut, it usually fell to the woodcutter or his current partner to meet their needs.

'What have I to give you?' thought the woodcutter, brushing aside the youngest hound, who had the friendliest of paws up on the woodcutter's broad shoulders. 'Is there a sheep in the cleit?' He walked to the cleit, which was close by the house, preceded by the wolfhounds.

This cleit, a kind of beehive hut, was a storeroom with a door. Like the woodcutter's hut, it was painstakingly built of two drystone skins. These skins, unlike the skins of the hut, which were packed with fine gravel, were packed with stones and covered with a tight-packed, more or less waterproof, roof of turf and wood. The stone walls were meant to admit wind but condense out moisture, so that meat could be hung to dry in the cleit without rotting away completely. While the system didn't work as effectively as once it might have, it was better than nothing. It probably worked quite well when the climate was warmer and drier than at present, but it was colder and wetter now than when the woodcutter's father began to build the hut. As well as meat, the woodcutter kept in the cleit his iron axe, his stone ard, his deer antler pick, his ox scapula shovel, and a saw, hammer, chisel, drill and square, all made of fine bronze. There were stones weighing down the roof, which nonetheless often blew off in a gale, and the ropes holding down the roof were made of twisted crowberry secured with gannets' beaks.

The woodcutter saw at once there was nothing in the cleit on which to feed the hounds. Nor was there any wood remaining to sell in order to buy meat. There was smoked meat in the roof of the hut but the hounds wouldn't eat smoked meat. He could have gone to one of his brothers' huts to borrow meat, but well he knew that his brothers' hounds, being fiercer than his own, would attack him if he did. He couldn't easily borrow a lamb from an outfield for the same reason, and so the woodcutter felt he had no choice but to go to the booley, a day's walk, and kill one of his own sheep or cattle and bring the meat back to his hut. His hounds certainly wouldn't hunt for themselves. Such meat as they could not eat would then serve as a stew for the woodcutter and his wife. Really, it was too bad no one had seen fit to warn him there was insufficient food and no wood, but then, he had been away longer than his family had anticipated.

Grabbing his crucifix and without telling his wife he was going off – he could hear her sobbing at the loom, where she was no doubt brooding over the king's beautiful daughter, whom she loathed – and sneaking away from the hounds, not that they would have followed anyway, the woodcutter set off in the last light of day to walk to the bothy on the booley. He hadn't gone but one hundred metres when he heard the ringing of the hand bell.

At first he wasn't sure it was a bell, as his smallest cockerel had a crow that sounded like a bell being rung. The woodcutter kept a dozen roosters, more than he needed to mate his hens, but under no circumstances would he tolerate the killing of a rooster. They died of old age, for the truth was, the woodcutter didn't like to get up in the mornings, and so needed at least a dozen roosters to make sure he didn't sleep in. Like his hounds, these roosters slept by the fire inside the hut.

He kept them only as alarm clocks. Eggs he could get from the cliff, and his wife preferred puffin and pigeon meat to chicken meat. In order to make a nourishing broth, she often boiled a puffin with a stone in a pot, and when the stone was sufficiently soft she threw away the puffin and the family drank the broth.

Yardbirds, hens and cockerels both, had come from Rome with Agricola. Parliament objected strongly to the yardbirds, on the ground that, like foxes and cats, they were not native to the Promised Land. But neither was parliament.

When the woodcutter heard the bell ring a second time he ran to the monastery and, sure enough, it was ringing from the window at the very top of the round tower. It was his fiancée! Good Lord, he had all but forgotten the Land where Stories End.

He crossed himself as he had seen pilgrims do, fetched the ladder from his cleit and climbed up to the round tower door, which, as well as being four metres off the ground, was bashed and battered about, by now, from the blows of eager suitors. To his dismay he found it locked. Then an executioner came along, wanting to know what he was up to. The woodcutter climbed down, returned the ladder to the cleit and ran all the way out to the king's palace, a broch with a walled garden, which stood not far from the clachan on a cliff over the sea.

The king was in his counting house counting out his pearls. The woodcutter asked if he might be admitted.

'Why, you miserable humbly,' said a guard. 'How could a poor fellow like you be admitted to the king's counting house? No one enters that counting house but only the king himself.'

'Who's that out there?' inquired the king over the rattle of black pearls.

'A bad-looking fellow,' replied the guard. 'Shall I call for an executioner?'

'No,' cried the woodcutter, 'it's me, Your Majesty. Me, your future son-in-law!'

'That you, Israel?' said the king. 'Just leave the key with the guard. I've locked the door to the tower again. They all still want to marry my girl. Just leave the key to the round tower door with the guard before you go off.'

As soon as the guard determined the woodcutter had no key on his person, he was seized and thrown in an oak barrique with his hands manacled together. This barrique resembled a wine cask, being a metre wide and a metre and a half long, with a hole down one side through which you could receive a bere bannock and water. Generally speaking, after a time in your barrique you determined not to eat, and later still not to drink, because your barrique was locked with strong locks which were never meant to be opened, so that wees and poos you did built up, until you could scarcely move. It was similar to, but even worse than, winter in a beehive hut.

Six executioners came and bore the barrique to a dungeon where they placed it on top of a second barrique and underneath a third. There were twenty or thirty barriques in the dungeon, all containing men, and as they did their wees and poos then died, the smell was bad.

The woodcutter wept as he was flung in a barrique, wept still louder when his barrique went into the dungeon, but the king was busy counting out his pearls, and the woodcutter's wife thought her husband was feeding his hounds, and the children were all at the bothy, so the woodcutter wasn't missed.

When, after a few weeks, he failed to return home, he was assumed by his brothers to have fallen off a cliff or drowned in a bog or been murdered by a thief. And after he'd been in his barrique a month his wife remarried, his children sold his livestock and split the estate among themselves, giving the cleit to his eldest son and the hut to his second wife, and his hounds moved in with his brothers' hounds. And after he'd been in his barrique two months, he was all but forgotten in the world. Only one person remembered him, or so he fancied, and that was the king's daughter. Her thoughts were with him, or so he conjectured. The king thought of him too, but only once in a while.

One evening, it must have been close on winter, the king came to the gaol, scouring the ground as usual for the key to the door to the tower. His sheriff had an easy job as no one could escape that gaol. The sheriff's duties consisted in feeding water and bere bannocks to the prisoners, such as wanted any, while identifying, from the smell, the recently deceased. It wasn't always easy to tell who was dead and who was not, as the smell was generally bad, so the sheriff spent a good deal of time just sniffing about the dungeon. He was in the process of training a pig to do this for him. When he heard the king, and he couldn't see the king, being blind from birth – it was a good job for a blind man, too, there being no light in the dungeon – it occurred to the sheriff this would be a chance to ask for a pay rise. He didn't earn much, just one black pearl a year. The sheriff couldn't recall the last time the king had paid a visit to the prison.

'God in Heaven,' said the king, 'is that my pig you have there?'

The sheriff explained to the king he was training the pig to sniff out the dead. Sniffing out dead bodies is a useful skill in an animal, so the king was impressed and inclined to forgive the sheriff for having stolen the pig. It was actually a wild pig but all wild pigs belonged to the king. 'Keep up the good work,' said the king, patting the pig on the snout. No sooner had the king's hand touched the pig's snout than the dutiful pig ran into the gaol and began sniffing the barriques.

'I'm here to inquire about a prisoner,' said the king. 'You had some woodcutters here. Would you know if the smallest is still alive? The smallest wood-cutter? None too bright?'

The sheriff declared he had no way of keeping records, not that they were needed as no one ever left the gaol. His main duty was to see which barrique contained a dead body. The king had to concede the system worked extremely well, as any barrique in which a prisoner died became, without modification, a coffin. It remained then only to dig a hole.

Normally, anyone who stepped out of line in the Promised Land was put to death, but once in a while lenience was shown in the handing down of a life sentence.

'We didn't ask to be born,' the king would say, 'which is why we look forward to being dead!' He said it in a loud voice so that prisoners could hear him and take comfort in his words.

'I locked my daughter in the round tower,' he confided to the sheriff, 'thinking the woodcutter had the key. It occurred to me, as I lay abed last night, unable to sleep for all the sinners researching the tower door, that the woodcutter may have swallowed the key, in which case it would still be in his barrique.'

'How long ago was this?' inquired the sheriff.

'I couldn't say,' said the king. 'Sometime over the past millenium. After the leprechauns came. After I lost my own key.'

The pig was indicating, with a high-pitched squeal, he had found a dead body. The sheriff, blind and unable to read or count, was youthful and willing, and soon had the barrique the pig had indicated free of the others. He pulled and tugged, while stacking barriques to either side of him as he worked, until he had a free-standing barrel before him, which he proceeded to open. As he'd never before been required to open a barrique he wasn't sure of how to do it, till eventually the king, concerned the barrique would be reduced to matchwood in the process, lent a hand. They soon had a few staves pulled off, but the stench was so bad the king passed out before he could examine the contents. When he came to, he found the sheriff up to his elbows in wees and poos.

'Don't waste time,' said the king, 'although I dare say you've plenty of it. The hide of you, to ask me for a one hundred per cent pay rise! You're lucky to have a job, as a handicapped person. I didn't ask you to do the search. You just fetch out the barrels. I'll conduct the search with my good eyes. Any man alive I shall address and I'd soon recognize that woodcutter. He speaks in a gruff voice like a puffin. I'm going back to my palace now to fetch me a scented handkerchief, so dislodge the barrels, quick as you like, and line them up for my inspection. Is it feeding time? Give them extra rations. No, don't give anyone extra rations.'

The king declared an amnesty, which was better than extra rations, releasing every prisoner he found alive in the gaol. This was the only amnesty ever declared in the Promised Land. And when eventually he came upon the woodcutter's coffin, which was the last to be removed, he thought he had another dead prisoner on his hands, because the woodcutter had his eyes tight shut and wouldn't speak, at first.

'I knew it was you,' said the king, 'as I've seen

every other villain here and none of them was as tough a nut as you. Won't you speak?'

'I'm content,' whispered the woodcutter, 'lying here in ecstasy and well I know that if I speak I'll soon be miserable again. I see the Land where Stories End, or so I conjecture.'

'The sheriff is after telling me you're off your food a month. You've not much life left in you. It's well I came along. I propose to release you, Israel, but first we're going to have a little chat.'

'Well now you have me talking so I feel my bliss depart.'

The king called on the sheriff and they opened the woodcutter's barrique. The poor woodcutter, hands unchained, was sat in a corner of the gaol as the king scrupulously searched through the wees and poos in the woodcutter's barrel.

'The fact you didn't want to leave your coffin,' said the king, 'is proof to me the key is here. Are you blind, Israel? A starving man dies blind, or so 'tis said.'

'I see you,' said the woodcutter, feeling the tingling warmth in his brain ebb down. This warmth is so composed the memory of it fades as the warmth fades.

'Ah,' said the king, 'what's this here I feel?' He held up something in his hand, but the clumsy sheriff inadvertently knocked his hand, causing what the king held to fall to the floor. It was the crucifix. With all those barrels being recently opened the floor was awash with wees and poos, so the king had no recourse but to dismiss the sheriff and mount a thorough search. As he worked through the wees and poos on the floor, he spoke to the woodcutter.

'I knew you had that key,' he said. 'Why can't you be honest with me? It's a shame, as well, you won't speak. This could be our best chance to get to know each other. I like to speak as I work. As I'm counting pearls I talk to myself. Did you know the Pope once came to visit here? Oh yes. This was before your time. He knew the Mystery of our True Faith is secured in the ruined tower and he wanted to be sure that no Muslim or Jew had access to it. "Don't worry your head," I said. "The Ruination of the Family, which is the Mystery of our True Faith, is perfectly safe with me. Am I not the man who built the tower and have I not lost the key?" His Holiness went back to Rome well satisfied that He who Mocks at All Good Things had no victory here to gloat over.'

'Then you and I are not the only men who found the key?'

'Any man can find the key. Every man in this kingdom can find the key, should he apply himself. Phoor! I need a drink! It's close in here. I'm going back to the broch to fetch me down a beer. Depend upon it, I'll have a good hunt for the key on the way there and back.'

When the king returned with beers he found the woodcutter standing. The woodcutter drank a bottle of beer then asked the king about the monastery.

'It was my home,' confided the king. 'My family owns that monastery. I'm hereditary abbot. We all had keys to the round tower, back in the good old days. My monks were killed in a raid, so in order to preserve the Mystery of our True Faith from the Old Enemy, I locked it in the tower. I guess it would be still there. I recall looking for it in the days when I had the key, but all I found were several oaken chests, containing pearls. I wasn't keen to ask about to see whose pearls they were, but when, after many years, no one came forward to claim them, I went to send them to the Pope, but before I could do so, the people, on seeing those pearls, insisted I be king. I guess they had the impression I might share the pearls with them, but I've no time for commoners. I simply cannot bear the silly way they stare at me. And you know, every time I count those pearls, I find I have more than before?'

'What about your daughter?'

'What about her? Don't ask so many questions. Say, why don't you look for the key to the door for a bit? After all, it's your key. From what I conclude there's always a man with a key and a boy who doesn't need a key. He'd be my true son and heir. Say, if I were to hold your body like this, can you work your arms? You're doing well. I like the smell of you. There's a touch of oak about you now, Israel. We all had that smell in the old days. There was an oak forest right here once, and choirs of boys, in oak stalls, singing hymns to us night and day. I confess I miss it.'

The woodcutter knew, from the mood he was in, he had lost his key to the door, so he didn't search too hard. True to his promise, the king eventually let the woodcutter go, then had the whole gaol searched by the sheriff, to no avail. During this search, the woodcutter paid a visit to his old clachan.

'If you want to marry Veronica,' said the king when the woodcutter returned, 'best confide what you did with the key. Alternatively, go back out to the island and refetch it.'

The woodcutter burst into tears.

'I don't want to marry your daughter,' he said. 'I see the folly of it now! I wanted to marry her once, that's true, but I don't want to marry her now. Why, look at what it cost me. All I want is to marry my own dear wife and she married another. Yes, when I went to my hut just now and knocked upon the door, a man answered who told me I no longer live there and my wife has remarried. But you know I was never dead.'

'I know nothing of the kind,' said the king, 'and I can't see what it has to do with me. On your way now Israel, and peace be with you.'

The King's
BEAUTIFUL
Kingdom

THE WOODCUTTER DIDN'T feel peaceful. He knew, by now, there was no peace in the Promised Land, not a bit of it. He resented having been interrupted by the king as he lay dying. Oh what peace and oh what bliss he had known in his barrique! He hadn't been lonely in the least. He hadn't been bored or fed up. He had the feeling the king's daughter had kept him company in his coffin.

If he thought hard, the woodcutter couldn't believe he would ever really die. Even though he had just been dying. What a waste it would be!

At the moment, he wanted to get back to his hut and sort out what had gone wrong, but something told him he would do better to wait till he had regained strength. Were a fight to break out, he could be taken advantage of, in his weakened condition. So he crawled off through a downy birch-wood by heather as brown as a buffalo's hide, towards a loch he could see in the distance, blazing away like a glob of mercury under a sun not anywhere apparent. As usual, the wind was whistling and howling over the snow-capped mountains, some with tops as sharp as pebble flints that threw up on the kingdom's beaches, others round as puddings, with scree spewing down, white-ribbed as a drunkard's tongue. When the woodcutter found a burn bubbling to a loch through paws of green moss, he pushed aside some flowering gorse, the tips of which a goat had been nibbling, and plunged in the burn, to stand and watch as sunlight struck a hill, making all the wet rocks, pools and puddles on the hill shine brightly. Later, when the last sunlight of day came down under low cloud, it caught in its rays both the white snow on the higher peaks and the white clouds behind them, so the woodcutter couldn't easily tell which of that white mass was snow and which was cloud. Overcome with a fresh appreciation for the beauties of the Promised Land, and realizing he had nowhere to sleep that night and nothing to eat, the woodcutter reached for his crucifix. To his horror he felt his chest bare. Had he left his crucifix in the barrique? Was it under the quern at home? He couldn't recall. Too exhausted to work out where it had gone, he fell asleep by the burn and dreamed a horrible dream, in which he did a dirty thing with a stranger.

Next morning he woke to find beside him a

venison haunch, half a dozen bottles of beer, the breast off a barnacle goose and an otter-fur cape. Apparently, the king had sent down a steward with some welcome food and drink and clothing. As the woodcutter tried on the cape, which was beautifully warm, with fine bone beads for buttons, he suddenly thought of how his wife and children would admire him in it, and burst into tears.

What was he to do? He didn't know where to begin to put his life back in order. He wasn't welcome in the king's palace without the key to the tower door and he felt reluctant to venture into the woods without the protection of his axe. He didn't like to return to his clachan until he had regained physical condition and hadn't the strength to walk through the snow to his bothy on the booley, to seek shelter there. He couldn't imagine beginning to build a new hut and a new cleit. It seemed to take more than one lifetime to complete the work involved. Why, he was still working on the hut his own father had bequeathed him and that hut was a long way from providing what a woman expected. Was the woodcutter destined to roam the kingdom as an anxious tramp, never certain of where he was to sleep or what he was to eat?

He recalled he had lost all fear when first he found that wretched key, and he also recalled that he hadn't really wanted to return to his family at the time. He would have been well content, back then, to have wandered as a traveller forever, even as he would have been well content to die in his oak barrique in the gaol. And while he didn't regret having been engaged to the king's lovely daughter, he did suspect his love for her had cost him his wife and his livestock. He'd realized for some time that while Veronica appeared normal, she was, perhaps unbeknown to her father, nothing of the kind. No normal girl could have laughed the way Veronica laughed when she emerged from the tower. Oh no, she was a fairy woman all right. He should have realized it sooner. Lying in his oak barrique where he'd had time to think these matters through, the woodcutter realized that a fairy woman has one advantage over a real one: because she comes from the Land where Stories End, you don't need to provide for her. Indeed, once you enter her bailiwick, she disappears. The love of one human being for another is a story, an ongoing story, and so belongs in the Promised Land, for there are no stories in the Land where Stories End. No one does a dirty thing so no one can be born there. No one eats bread there and no one drinks beer. No one ages in the Land where Stories End. No one dies. No one laughs or cries or shouts. It is indeed a truly happy land, for stories are either boring – as when people live happily ever after – or tragic, as when they don't.

Next day the cloud was like a knife edge and there was heavy frost on the ground. The woodcutter, weary in his mind because of the privations he had endured, ate the last of his venison haunch and walked off into the sunlight. The snow was gleaming on the mountain tops and everything was washed clean because it had rained hard the previous afternoon. The woodcutter paused to admire the colour in a mallard drake's green-feathered head. Thank you, he said, but no sooner had he said it, than he wondered whom he was thanking.

Was it the king? No, because, although the king owned the drake, he had all those pearls he never meant to share. You wouldn't thank him for anything. And the woodcutter felt sure of one thing: it wasn't a man he was thanking. It wasn't the king's daughter, because she was a fairy. You had to be careful of her. Although she could be a comforter, she had cost the poor woodcutter everything he owned. It couldn't be the woodcutter's current partner, as she was betrothed to another, and he would have a few sharp words to say to her when next they met. It couldn't be his daughters either, as all they ever did was mock him. He was thoroughly fed up with defending his own good taste in music against theirs. It couldn't be a person who could tear you limb from limb. You had to be as careful with a witch as you were with any fairy woman. It couldn't be that pert cellar maid, of whom, for some reason, he grew fonder all the time. He hadn't seen her in twenty years. For the same reason, time elapsed, it couldn't be his first wife, he didn't think.

Could it be one of his brothers' wives? Probably not. They hated him.

What about that deaf old woman who lived in the hut on the Edge of the World? By midday the woodcutter had considered, only to eliminate, every woman but one. In the end, he realized it had to be his own mother he was thanking. After all, she was the person who had introduced him to the world: it made good sense to thank her for everything in it he admired. There was still the problem of time elapsed, for how long since he'd seen his own mother? It was more than twenty years.

Worn out from cogitation, the woodcutter came to a beach where the smooth, grey stones made a chirring, scratching rattle as the waves mounted the shore. A pair of grey seals and a pilot whale cavorted in the sea a little way off. The shores in this part of the kingdom were sandy mud or acres of stones. If he kept to the shoreline, the woodcutter knew he was sure to encounter the woodheap, and without an axe he had no way to earn his living any more. He needed to find wood if he meant to eat bread and drink beer.

Mind you, he wasn't completely sure he wanted to regain strength. He had quite enjoyed his month without a meal, towards the end. But every hour or so now, when it started to rain, he wished he were dead. Looking down at his own bones, off which the freckled skin was hanging loosely, and shivering, because he was now so thin even his fine fur cape couldn't keep him warm, he would groan and throw himself to the ground, cursing his mother for having given him birth.

But then it would stop raining, as the wind blew away the cloud that had caused the shower, and the puddles on the water would dimple in the wind, and the woodcutter would sit up to see water everywhere, white in the waves and waterfalls, black or brown in the deeper pools and burns, turquoise green over the sand in a bay, or deep blue, under the deep blue sky at sea, and every bit of grass and heather and gorse and downy birch atoss in the wind, and then he would feel brave and confident and optimistic, and thank his mother for having given him birth.

Five swans in the reeds of a freshwater tarn were paddling about. The woodcutter watched them wiggling their black, webbed feet as they upended themselves. One honked at the others in warning as the woodcutter approached.

'Don't mind me,' said the woodcutter. 'I'm thanking my mother you exist. After all, she gave me the chance to observe you, lovely white creatures that you are. If I had never been born, I could scarcely be standing here now, admiring you. And come to think of it, isn't that all we do in the Land where Stories End? Look about us?'

All thought of the Land where Stories End departed the woodcutter's mind the minute he saw the activity taking place by the ruined abbey. A large wooden boat was sitting offshore, with a currach tendering to it, and a pair of men were about to load the last of the woodheap on the currach. The rest was already aboard the big boat.

'Hey,' shouted the woodcutter, 'get your hands off

that wood! *I* am the first man to see that wood. It doesn't belong to you!'

The men, one of whom had a hooked nose and a bald pate and the other a scrawny neck, took no notice of the woodcutter and hardly bothered looking up from their work. Like most men in the kingdom, they too had tried to open the door to the tower, but one failed effort had wisely dissuaded them from attempting a second.

Holding tightly in his iron grip his sole remaining beer bottle, the woodcutter ran, fast as he could, over the sandy dunes of the machair. He was struggling to walk and gasping for breath when he reached the two perpetrators of the theft, so that they laughed at his discomposure.

The woodcutter lost his temper. The nerve of these men, to steal his wood! He jumped in, swinging with the beer bottle, but soon discovered he was not his old self. In fact, these thieves had no trouble pushing him over, time and again.

'Keep out of our way,' said one thief eventually. 'Find someone else to annoy.'

'Yes that's right,' said the second thief. 'Take a running jump at yourself. There's plenty of peat in the kingdom if you must have a cooked meal. Personally, I find a piece of raw whale blubber makes a tasty snack.'

'Show me mercy,' whined the woodcutter. 'Must you grab the whole heap?'

'Why should we leave wood for you? You're no one special to us.'

'I'm a man same as you and I'm going through a bad patch! I just lost all my possessions. If you don't leave me a piece of wood then I've no way to buy beer and bread.'

'You don't look poor to us. Not when you're wearing that fine fur cape far better than ever we owned. Why, there's good as oaks as ever were cut right there in the forest behind you. Sell that cape and buy an axe, for if you're too lazy to cut down trees you deserve to starve and sleep sober. Think yourself lucky we don't kill you and take the cape for our children.'

Clutching his cape the woodcutter sprawled on the sand to consider his position. He'd never in his life been beaten in a fight as he always chose his opposition carefully. To anyone younger or stronger or larger than himself he avoided giving offence, whereas old, weak and diminutive people could feel the full strength of his displeasure. This pair, in his prime, he would have vanquished, he felt certain, but things had changed. He now felt obliged to give them a smile and thank them for their consideration.

'Am I that man,' he wondered, watching the boat make off with his wood, 'who just a day or so ago was willing, nay eager, to die? Can I believe, that in fear of my life, I backed down from those thieves? What in God's name has happened to me, between then and now? I was all set ready to die, in the barrique, and in fact, quite looking forward to it, yet my heart was just now beating so that I could scarcely swallow or breathe.'

A

CONFLUX

of

THREE

Roads

FOR A TIME he sat on the iris, sniffing the bromide smell of the weeds and looking out to sea to where he'd seen the Land where Stories End. When he turned towards the deaf old woman's hut, thinking he might quiz her, it was gone. All the huts in the village had gone, cannibalized, he supposed. All that remained of the village on the Edge of the World were the abbey ruins.

The sun set on a dark and stormy night. The woodcutter hauled himself to his feet, picked up his bottle of beer, fastened the buttons on his otter-fur cape and trudged off into the forest. He took care to avoid the route he knew would lead him to the witch's lair, for he couldn't be sure of how she would react to an otter-fur cape. She might try to grab it.

The wych-elm, the rowan, the downy birch and the sessile oak were leafless, but the forest was mainly oak, covered in filmy fern and often as not with ivy, the great buttresses of the roots clinging to the sandstone rocks. The woodcutter walked till he could walk no further, then sprawled under an oak to rest. To his surprise he saw that, while all the other oaks had lost their leaves, this one had leaves attached. Looking up in the moonlight, he saw a great mass of fluttering gold, but the leaves dropped on him as he lay down under the tree. A torrent of leaves fell on him, though there wasn't any breeze right then, so the woodcutter soon had a comfortable bed on which to spend the night. It was metres deep, dry and warm, and a long way from the nearest prickly holly bush.

As he lay on the couch he had been providentially provided, he held up the bottle of beer, which was all the sustenance he had left. It looked lovely in the moonlight, with a glow to the grooved clay pot, but he threw it away as far as he could. He wasn't thirsty and didn't want to have to get up in the night to do a wees. As it came from the royal brewery, this beer, you can be sure it was a strong drop.

At once a leprechaun appeared, holding a seal-oil lamp. He jumped up on the oak-leaf couch as nimble as a deer.

'What are you doing here?' he said. 'I hope you don't mean to cut this tree down!'

'Not a bit of it,' said the woodcutter. 'As you can

see I've no axe. I've just been visiting a close-by ruined village that is dear to my heart, and you know there was a woodheap there, but two men stole the wood?'

'Haven't I seen you before?' asked the leprechaun. 'Yes, I thought I had! You're the man who was looking to find the key to the door to the tower. You know, the round tower where the king's daughter's locked up?'

'Acting on your advice I found the key and released the king's daughter, but then I lost the key again and now the king has locked her back up. So you're right to describe her as locked up.'

'What? You found the key to the door but then you lost it?'

'I did,' confessed the woodcutter, 'and tell you what, it's easily done. Why, did not the king himself lose the key to the door?'

'I suppose you want it back?'

'I'm not sure. As to marrying the king's daughter, the girl is a fairy woman.'

'Of course she is a fairy woman. Did you not fall in love with her?'

'Of course I fell in love with her! Every man in the kingdom is in love with the king's daughter. It won't work, as my wife was never happy when I was with the lass, especially resenting the bere bannocks I prepared for her on Fridays. You see, she wouldn't eat them.'

'How could she eat them? Fairy women don't eat but they do appreciate a gesture. Now what's this about a wife?'

'My current partner, the mother of my seventeen children, though she went off with another. She only did that because she thought I was dead when I am not. Can you help me get her back?'

The leprechaun flew in a temper and stamped the leaves with his winklepicker shoes.

'No man who has seen the Land where Stories End should have a wife for where would be the good of a wife to a man who can do no dirty thing?'

'Hold your tongue,' said the woodcutter. 'I have done a dirty thing since I was back from there and don't presume to lecture me about the Promised Land. We human beings understand it better than a leprechaun. In fact, I can give you any advice on cows or bees you may need.'

'Shame on you,' said the leprechaun. 'A married man had no right to seek the Land where Stories End. You have now lost your way between the World of the Flesh and the Spirit World. I should seek, if I were you, instructions from a saint, for surely your soul is in peril. You could become a great sinner.'

'Think so?' The woodcutter was not a little pleased. 'I doubt I've the strength for it. But I do appreciate advice and am always bearing it in mind. Right now, I need to punish this bully who stole my hut.'

'From an ass to a philosopher and back to an ass,' laughed the leprechaun, 'with the aid of the Virgin's Milk. You stole a taste but the only way you were going to get a taste was to steal one. Peace be with you.'

Then he disappeared. Suddenly, as always.

'What was that about,' thought the woodcutter. He lay on his back then upon his belly, curled up to one side then turned upon the other, but no matter which way he lay that night, he just couldn't seem to get to sleep. In the end he got up, found the bottle of beer he'd thrown away in good faith, skolled it and fell in a stupor. It was more a barley wine, that beer from the royal brewery.

Some time later that night the woodcutter was woken by a terrible noise. Three ogres were crashing through the forest, making a windstorm that blew away all the leaves on the oak-leaf couch. Horrified at the thought of being quizzed again by ogres, the woodcutter curled into a tight ball and hid in a hollow of the great oak tree, hoping they wouldn't see him there, and they didn't, at first. They did stop outside the tree, so the woodcutter could hear every word they said, although his heart was beating so loudly he thought they could probably hear it. They probably could, as ogres have an excellent sense of hearing, a sense that matches perfectly their excellent sense of smell. They can hear as well as bats as well as smell as well as dogs, but luckily for certain folk they can't see all that flash.

'Phew,' said the biggest, ugliest ogre, 'pass us that thermos of blood, would you lads? Ah, t'at's grand. T'at's loovely. What a night we've had so far and the night has just begun.'

'I enjoyed holding the little girl's head under water,' said the third ogre. The woodcutter recognized him from his whining, querulous voice. Then the second ogre, the one with the eagle claws and the bull's head, spoke. When he coughed, he turned his head toward the oak to be polite, and the sulphurous smoke from his breath quite filled the woodcutter's hideout, tickling his throat.

'Why,' said the second ogre, 'do people feel they never need pay for all the pain that they have caused? Take that little girl tonight, the one we drowned, she looked surprised to me. Even though she was just a little thing, no more than ten years of age, did she honestly suppose she could eat all those salmon, every one of which was taken from the water by her father, without herself having, at some stage, to breathe in water as those poor fish were forced to breathe in air? What do their parents teach them these days?'

'I like to see their surprise,' said the third ogre. 'It's what I live for. I loathe these filthy creatures that do these wees and poos and am always disappointed when they know what to expect as they die. It spoils my fun. That's why I'm glad to see the monks being killed and the abbeys falling down. The monks were bent on turning people into trees. I begrudged them that ambition.'

'I don't like Christians,' confessed the first ogre. 'Where do they come from, these Christians? When first I come here from over the seas there was not a Christian to be seen. I had plenty of work then. But

Christians go round confessing their sins to the point they want to kiss me, some of them! Oo, I don't like that.'

'They were drowning and reviving them in these baptisms and as they only ate the fish, that left me as little work as yourself,' complained the second ogre.

'They had the Secret of the Oak,' said the third ogre 'which I suspect they got from the druids, when the druids went over to their side. Whilst ever they had the Secret of the Oak they had access to the Land where Stories End. I could scarcely pursue them there. But I notice Christians are cutting down oaks today as fast as they can, and they haven't burnt a criminal in a wicker basket in years, or lit a sacred flame.'

'Yes, it's going pretty well,' admitted the first ogre. 'Pass us that thermos of ... just a minute – did I hear someone sneeze? That sounded like a mortal sneeze, full of dirty things.'

Sure enough, the woodcutter had had to stifle a sneeze and the first ogre's sharp ears had picked this up. He lit a torch, skolled his cup of blood, then dragged the woodcutter out from where he was hiding, by the bone buttons on the otter-fur cape.

'Well, if it's not our pilgrim,' he remarked. 'And what brings you into the woods at night again?'

'Cut him up with his axe,' said the third ogre. 'Don't waste further time on him. Far from being a pilgrim, as he claimed, he is in fact a killer of the oak. The spirits of all the oaks he has killed are waiting for him.

I shouldn't be in his shoes.'

Now when you're dealing with ogres, as the wood-cutter knew, it's best to get on the front foot, especially if you've no breastplate with which to protect yourself.

'If people like me don't build the odd clearing,' he argued cogently, 'where are men to sow corn? How are cattle and sheep to fatten if all the grass is in the shade? How are men to build roofs and make charcoal for met-alwork if there's no wood? It may be cruel to thin oak, though some would argue to the contrary, but any ani-mal husbandman knows that sheep and cattle like a bit of grass.'

'Do they? The men who were here when first I come,' said the first ogre, spinning the bone in his nose, 'would never have dreamed of cutting down a tree, and such axes as they had were made of stone and they only used them on each other. They always expected to see me, they told me the gospel truth, and they took such punishments as I meted out to them without complain-ing to their mothers.'

'But did they kill animals?' inquired the third ogre, who was a bit younger than the others.

'They did,' affirmed the second ogre. It was his duty to punish such men as offended the animal king-dom. 'They killed them but they didn't first enslave and love them, so they'd less to fear from me.'

'This was all before my time,' explained the third ogre. 'I find it fascinating.' He then turned to the woodcutter.

'Is it true,' he asked, 'that in cities, people eat meat and burn wood all day?'

'Don't ask me,' said the woodcutter. 'I never saw a city.'

'But aren't you off to Rome? We supposed that being a pilgrim, you'd be on your way to Rome.'

'No, I'm going home,' declared the woodcutter. 'Over that hill there, beyond the sacred well, I've a wife and seventeen children.'

'Good lad,' exclaimed the first ogre. 'Why, you're not as bad as you appear. Now tell me, have you caused any pain to a human being since last we met?'

The woodcutter thought at once of his poor dear mother and burst into tears.

'I've long neglected my mother,' he wailed. 'I've been a neglectful son!'

The first ogre doubted the woodcutter's mother would miss him as much as he missed her.

'No further questions,' he declared. 'It's over to you now, comrades.'

The second ogre asked had the woodcutter been unkind to an animal. He had to confess he'd eaten quite a few, so the second ogre said he would need to be punished for this. Then the third ogre, the one who looked like a gum tree, asked had he cut any trees down, but as he hadn't, it was up to the second ogre to decide his punishment.

'How many animals would you say you've eaten?' inquired the second ogre.

'I don't know,' said the woodcutter. 'Ten or perhaps twenty.'

'Then what say I reach up your bum with my eagle claw here and pull out your liver and lights, then hand them over to my one-eyed colleague to eat, ten or twenty times?'

The first time he did it, the woodcutter thought the pain couldn't get worse. But the sixth time he screamed for his mother so loudly his mother actually heard. So did everyone else in the Promised Land. Yes, the poor woodcutter's elderly mother was still alive, living alone in a stalled cairn, but she was too weak and feeble with age to come to her son's assistance.

As the first ogre was gobbling up the woodcutter's liver and lights the ninth time, the third ogre noticed a droplet of white blood among the red blood dribbling down his colleague's chins. At this, all three ogres exchanged a quick glance, stubbed out their torches, drained their cups of blood, and stormed off to find another victim.

Thinking it had been a dreadful nightmare, the woodcutter did a wees and went back to sleep. But when he awoke, there was his liver and lights all over his otter-fur cape. He had no choice but to shove them up his own bum, before moving on.

'Why is it so dark and stormy?' he growled. No one ever seeks to walk the dark and stormy road. In this, the dark and stormy road is like the bright and sunny one. Only those who walk the dry and dusty road select their road. So far as they're concerned it is the only road there is, because that's what the first sign they always see must always say. Remind yourselves of this before we meet the dry and dusty road, which soon enough we shall, but we shan't be walking it, scout's honour.

Thoroughly wet and dispirited and sore in his back, crack and sac, the woodcutter was soon in a part of the forest he'd never before seen. There was quite a lot of forest the woodcutter hadn't seen, but bear in mind that most of the kingdom was still covered in trees, and people who wanted to travel about usually did so by boat.

Today, the place is deforested and that's what makes the music so sad. It has nothing to do with the fact the people are always fighting each other.

The trees in this part of the kingdom were pines and growing so closely together, a strongly built wood-cutter could barely squeeze between. The thick-trunked trees provoked each other fiercely with straight, out-thrust limbs.

The woodcutter had lost the path, and as the sun grew darker and the rain heavier, and the bark of the pine trees began to chafe and itch and cut his arms, he suddenly wished that he were dead, and flung himself down on the ground in a sulk.

'Isn't it a shocking thing entirely,' he reflected, 'that those robbers took my wood. And isn't it dreadful I have lost my wife and family through no fault of my own. Poor fellow! What will become of my wolfhounds and my fine cattle and sheep? What of my famous cockerels? What of my carpentry set? How I wish I'd never gone in search of the key to the door, for the fact is, I have not had a minute's peace of mind ever since. Not even one black pearl have I gained through my activities, but only the loss of everything I owned in the Promised Land. Well, maybe I should get up and go on, if only to warn others not to heed a leprechaun's advice. But that would mean lifting my head and flexing my limbs and I couldn't be bothered. No, I'm just going to lie here, feeling sorry for myself, until the mud drowns me, or the pine needles cover me completely, or the pine martens eat me.'

So the woodcutter lay a good ten minutes, till a sound came to his ears of weeping and wailing and gnashing teeth. It wasn't far off. He tried to ignore it, but his curiosity soon got the better of him, and it wasn't long before he was up on his feet and running towards the sound.

There was a clearing and in this clearing a group of travellers sprawled out. They'd built a campfire but the fire wasn't burning well, even though a couple of children were heaping it with damp wood. To keep a campfire burning on a wet night with rain pouring down, you needed to be, as the woodcutter was, an expert fire-setter. Seeing these poor travellers, many of them shivering as they wept and wailed, and keen to see a fire going, if only to warm his own back, crack and sac, the woodcutter showed the little children how to set a proper fire. Then he took two flints from where he kept them, in the depths of his beard, and soon had a fire blazing away despite the torrential rain. With light from the fire to guide him he turned to see what the weeping was about, and it was then he realized that most of these adult travellers were very ill. They had the plague. Their hands and faces erupted in weeping sores, and some of them coughed like old wethers.

'Children will die,' wailed a bald-headed piece. The woodcutter recognized her. Why, she was one of those travellers from the clearing where he'd first found the crucifix. Recalling how rude she'd been to him, he thought of kicking out the fire again, but compassion for the children and the thought of his own welfare prevented him from doing this. Eventually, he dragged one bald-headed woman towards the fire, then gave the chief, who was the biggest and ugliest and sickest, his otter-fur cape. It was only for a lend. This left him naked, but these women were too ill to be impressed by a naked man.

'They want to find a priest to shrive them,' said a happy lad. The woodcutter wasn't sure he was a boy until he had seen him do a wees.

'What do you mean?' said the woodcutter, hoping not to appear stupid. The fact was, he didn't know much about the Christian faith. He was no churchgoer.

'All these women,' continued the boy, with a smile, 'are mostly dead. Even my own dear mother' – and he pointed at the chief – 'has lost her wife.'

The woodcutter, thinking at once of his own dear mother, was moved to tears. He felt sorry the chief of the women had lost her loving wife, and as the fire was now going well, he decided to fetch the priest, even though he didn't understand what it meant to be 'shriven' and didn't like the sound of it.

From the corner of his eye, he could see quite a few bottles of beer, and these would adequately recompense him for his efforts, were these successful. So snatching back the cape and filling its pockets with bottles of beer, as many as would fit, the woodcutter advised the children on how to keep the fire going in his absence, then set off into the dark and stormy woods, as he imagined, quite alone. He hadn't gone far when he saw the boy who had spoken to him, following. The child was all but naked, and his white skin shone in the light of the torch the woodcutter was carrying, in the hope of fending off wild beasts. It must have worked, too, as he'd never so much as seen a wild beast in the forest.

'What are you on about?' said the woodcutter. 'Who invited you? How can you skip and smile and sing when your poor mother lies dying? For all her faults she *is* your mother. There's no chance I'll find a priest, as I don't even know where I am, so don't waste time tagging along. You go back to the clearing.'

The boy kept his distance. Indeed, he was pretty nimble. He seldom did as he was bidden either, having been spoiled by his mother and her wife.

'Didn't you hear what I just said? You go back to your mother!'

The woodcutter didn't like this boy, who seemed too debonair in a world of thieves and plague and injustice. If only I had my axe, he thought, I could gain respect from the boy. As things stand, I best go back and return the wretch to his mother.

'Come on,' he said to the boy, and the boy followed after him, laughing all the way.

When they got back they found the chief of the women purple in the gills. A couple of her bald-headed friends, with rings through their noses, were trying to support her. Seeing the child, the chief called out with the last breath she would draw.

'Galahad!' she cried. 'O Galahad, come here and put your arms around your dying mother. Certain it is that when we're dead we're dead, as though we'd never existed. It is too late now to fetch a priest, for I must join my own dear heart, but I have a truth I must confess, as I find, to my surprise, I have a conscience. Galahad, you are not, as I have claimed, the son of my wife and myself. Rather, you are the son of myself with the king of the Promised Land. When I was a young nun, living outside the wall to the old monastery, the king did a dirty thing to me and you are the fruit of the dirty thing he did. Oh I'm fearful of what the king may do, should he learn he has a son, so don't you mention it to a soul. Above all, don't tell the king, for certain it is he will imprison or kill you. Never was a more miserable, cruel man born, unless it were the Pope.'

But before the boy could promise a thing, his mother died and that was the end of her.

The woodcutter felt he might care for the child and protect him, as necessary, from the king. Once the secret of this birth was out, the boy would certainly be in danger, and the woodcutter knew he couldn't keep a secret like this to himself, and he was right. He felt he was bound to tell the first person he encountered, which is just what he did. And now he thought of it, the way the child conducted himself suggested royal parentage. Galahad was always singing and skipping, as though he meant to live forever. He hadn't a care.

The woodcutter didn't really blame the child for not being upset by his mother's death. She was a frightful creature with a very bad reputation. But surely the fact he now knew his father was king of the kingdom should have caused him to rejoice? The woodcutter pointed out, over and again, what it meant in terms of black pearls, but the boy just laughed and asked what possible use was a black pearl to anyone.

'I can see you've had a poor education,' said the woodcutter, leaving it at that.

'You know,' he said later, making light conversation as together they squeezed through the hazel, 'I slept last night on a comfortable bed. It would have been one of the best sleeps ever I had, except for three ogres. I generally sleep on bracken beneath a skin I didn't properly tan, surrounded by roosters and above me a roof that tends, as roofs do, to leak.'

'Why live indoors?' inquired the boy. 'Why sleep by night and waste time? When my dear mother and her wife, God rest their souls, slept, I looked on.'

'It's clear to me,' said the woodcutter, 'you've never done a day's hard work, my lad, for if you had, you would understand the benefits of sleep. The best part of any day is when we're falling asleep at night, for it's then we know another day is over and there's one fewer left to endure.'

'But sleeping people bark and snort and whimper, just like dogs!'

'Those women, I suspect, dreamt of men,' said the woodcutter, blowing out his torch as the sun rose, 'but if you think you can go through life without once shutting your eyes, think again. We build ourselves by dreaming. Deprived of sleep we forget who we are. Besides, I won't keep an idle lad. You'll be working hard. You'll sharpen my axe and carry wood. Imagine having no break at all between one day and the next! How awful! Life would just go on and on and it's bad enough as is. Another thing, I won't have you sitting by, staring at me when I'm sleeping. I bray like an ass and my mouth falls open, or so I have been told. Who's to say you won't go through my sporran in search of pearls? The more hours a man sleeps the better he feels in the morning. I half suspect that half-sister of yours sleeps night and day. There'd be nothing else for her to do in that round tower. I know she's fond of me, too, although she never speaks a word. If I could just find the key to the door, I might yet marry her, I don't know. I haven't properly decided. Frankly, I didn't think there'd be so many complications. Now we'll start tonight. You will sleep for an hour, my lad, after I have shown you how it's done.'

Galahad fell in a sulk and was trudging along head down, when suddenly they came to a clearing. It was the clearing, looking the worse for wear, in which lived the dark witch.

The black cow had a white calf at foot, and was grazing on what grass she could find, but there wasn't much grass left in the meadow. The woodcutter, seeing where he was, went straight back into the forest.

'Wait!' cried the boy. 'Here's a friendly cow and a river to swim in. Can't we remain?'

'Another meadow and we might, but here lives a wicked witch who preys on innocence. Why, she once tore me limb from limb!'

'Is she young with long black hair? If so, I know her name. I like her, too. We'd often camp in this meadow. Do you want to know her name?'

'Ssshh!' The woodcutter pushed his fingers in his ears, as far as they would fit. He knew if you know the name of a witch you can call her up and she might come. Well, the woodcutter didn't want that happening as he had trouble enough with women. All he wanted, now he had regained strength, was to reclaim his wife.

God, how he missed her!

While he was brooding over his wife, the boy ran into the clearing. The calf, delighted to meet a youngster with whom to romp, was soon playing head-butts. An old cow makes for dull company, as she only wants to play one day in every twenty-one.

The woodcutter knew his way home from here, and while it was a lovely meadow, it was less appealing with the oak tree gone and the heather taking over. When hired to construct a meadow, it was the woodcutter's practice to take a walk first, discover the biggest oak about, then construct the clearing around it.

Sprawled out as he waited for the boy, he recalled the swim he had taken in the river, during which time he had asked Christ to wash him clean of sin. Well, if he was going to be a pilgrim, he'd reasoned he ought to get a bit of practice in. But now there was no tree at all off which to hang to bathe. Someone was cutting down the trees and ruining the look of the meadows he had built. Likely as not, that pile of wood, by the seashore, had come from such trees. They were the easiest to fall.

The woodcutter might have grown indignant, except it was so warm on the edge of the clearing, he soon fell sound asleep. He was smiling, dreaming of watching his wife's delight on being introduced to a new son, when a monk sneaked up behind him and kicked him softly, with a foot.

'Ho there fellow,' said the monk.

The woodcutter jumped up, reaching for an axe

that wasn't there, but soon relaxing, when he saw it was only a monk and not a thief or a leprechaun. The monk was wearing a dressing gown and clutching a cross, all dusty and dry.

Seeing the cross, the woodcutter crossed himself as he had seen pilgrims do. Whereupon the monk pulled out a bere bannock and broke it in half. The woodcutter wanted to break off a piece from his own chunk and give it to the boy, but he was a big man with a big appetite, and before he knew it there was none left.

'What brings you into the woods?' asked the monk as he ate his own bread, or what passed for bread in those parts. He kept glancing over his shoulder as if expecting company.

Eager, as always, to speak of himself to anyone who might listen, the woodcutter told of how the boy in the clearing was actually the king's son, and of how he, the woodcutter, had searched for the key to the door to the tower, and of how he had met a leprechaun, twice, and of how this leprechaun had given him bad advice, as it turned out, and of how his wife didn't approve at all of the king's daughter, and of how, in consequence, Veronica had lost her laugh, and of how he had lost his key to the door, and of how three ogres had quizzed him, twice, and all the while the monk listened. The woodcutter never mentioned his journey to the Land where Stories End, for the reason he had forgotten his journey to the Land where Stories End. It was a very square peg indeed in the round hole of his experience.

The more he talked the more he found he longed for his own dear wife. He'd quite forgotten his mother, and didn't like to tell the monk about the witch.

'What a capable woman is that wife of mine,' boasted the woodcutter. 'How she can cook and sew! She's always able to make ends meet, even if there's no wood, and she never forgot to lock up the yardbirds. No fox ever got them.' He didn't dare speak of what he most missed in a wife, of course. Not to a monk.

In fact, this monk had been a family man and would have understood. There were monks, in the Promised Land, with wives and families of their own. There were even monks who stole sheep and cattle from other monasteries, behaviour towards which many a venal abbot would turn a blind eye.

Finally, the monk wearied of hearing about the woodcutter's wife and ended the conversation by asking a very difficult question.

'Tell me,' he said, 'is there anything about this woman that you *don't* like?'

The woodcutter was still thinking of an answer when some more monks appeared. There were ten or more of them, scholars, led by the saint we already met. The saint's presence had its usual impact on the sinner, but as he fell to his knees the woodcutter finally thought of the answer, and so the first words the saint heard the woodcutter say were, 'I don't like the way she laughs.'

The
DRY
and
DUSTY
Road

YOU MIGHT THINK it strange, a woodcutter meeting a saint, but the Promised Land had saints by the score in the days before cars and telly. Every part of the kingdom had a saint. Some had two, which meant supernumerary saints had to sail off to unknown parts. They were a peripatetic lot, familiar with icebergs and volcanoes. Some lived alone as hermits, while others were cenobites, like Finn.

Finn was the saint who had saved the woodcutter from Galahad's mother. He probably didn't remember that but I hope you do. If not, it might be better for you to go back and start the book again. The minute Finn appeared among them, people forgot their grievances, for saints see right through your liver and lights into the depths of your being. What they see there is your soul wrapped in your personality, that is, something resembling a pearl surrounded by an oyster of ignorance and misery.

Finn liked his monks to construct the most beautiful books on the skins of young calves. These books concerned what Jesus Christ had had to say to the fairy folk, a subject on which Finn, at that time, was the world's greatest expert. Nothing like these books had ever been seen in the Promised Land, and while most people couldn't read they did admire illustrations, affording Finn the pretext of educating them in Christ. While people's attention was diverted as they admired the multicoloured letters in the books, Finn would gently lead them on the dry and dusty road. And that is a road, we are assured, that has never failed an honest heart.

'Tell me about yourself,' said Finn, 'but make it brief I pray. We have many a mile to walk before we rest this day.'

It wasn't one of Finn's better days. Nor was he looking, as he spoke, at the woodcutter whom he addressed. As he assisted the contrite woodcutter off his massive knees, Finn looked to where the pale boy was playing head-butts with the white calf. And as he gazed, Finn's scarred face assumed an eagle's glare, for here was a man who sensed at once this boy's special promise.

Overcome with the feeling of relief men often report when they meet a saint, a feeling some liken to a spigot being pulled from a barrique of wees and poos, the woodcutter hastened to recount his life in the customary sequence. He hadn't gotten to his first meeting with the leprechaun when the saint raised a hand, and when a saint raises a hand, ignorant folk fall silent. It should be recalled the woodcutter had actually been a saint himself, for a bit, but folk on the dark and stormy road are torn this way and that, and as often reduced to the level of an ass as joined in union with The One. Such is the nature of the dark and stormy road. Think hard before you persist with it. If only the woodcutter could have retained his key or even his crucifix, he might have been able to speak with the saint of what he'd seen in the Land where Stories End. Unfortunately, that land was a fast fading memory to the woodcutter, a glib tale that lost more lustre each time it was told. Why, it even slipped the poor woodcutter's mind completely, on occasion. At present, he was more inclined to focus on how he'd lost his carpentry set. The monk to whom he had been speaking, the monk who had given him the bread, whispered something in Finn's ear, and Finn nodded, though never once taking his eyes off the boy Galahad.

'We are all sons of the king,' said Finn, 'for such is our curse and our blessing. But our king is ill and we cannot make him well through our undressing.'

At this point, he pulled out a bere bannock, broke it and offered it to his monks. It was rare to see a saint eat, as they deprive themselves of food and sleep.

'I wouldn't mind a bite of that,' said the woodcutter, miffed he hadn't been offered any. 'In exchange I'll tell you about this meadow, which is not as it appears. A witch lives here and I was thinking of her as you spoke, my friend, for like yourself she wants to cure the king but she would do it by undressing. I wonder where she can be? She tells me she never leaves the clearing.'

The saint whispered something to a monk who wore his long hair in a mullet, before wandering off to the river to pray up to his neck in cold running water. Another monk then asked what had been said in order to write it down, for everything the saint said was dutifully written down.

'He says we cannot see her as no woman can be three. No woman, says Finn, can be a saint's daughter, a maiden's mother and a fool's confidante. He says she's in the king's pay and that each full moon a steward comes here, to pay her one black pearl.'

'Then let us,' said the woodcutter, rising, 'let us look for her treasure trove, for she told me, may God be my witness, she never leaves the clearing. We have men enough here to mount a thorough search, so let's begin. There's nowhere here she could have spent that treasure trove. You start here, sir. And you start there, sir, and I'll start here.'

'Wait,' said the monk with the mullet, 'you haven't heard the full story. Before taking her pearl, she demands it dissolved in red wine then drinks it down her.'

'Drinks it *down* her?' The woodcutter couldn't believe his ears. Certainly, there was no point in mounting a search for pearl.

Finn was in the river, up to his head in the cold flowing water. They watched him raise his arms over his head as he asked The Lord for guidance.

'Look!' said a monk, and when they looked, there was the boy, sucking on the cow. Inspired by the calf, he would then butt the cow's bag in order to increase the flow and, as he did, the calf, on the other side of the cow, would do the same.

'You'd think they were meant to suckle four,' observed a monk, 'for see how they have four quarters? Goats have only two.'

'Like your dam,' came the jibe, and the monks again laughed heartily. The woodcutter hadn't thought these holy men would be so brash. He felt both let down and disappointed, partly because of their unseemly levity, mostly because that stupid witch had pissed away all those pearls. If it was meant as an effort to cure the king it was certain to fail, for had not the king himself told the woodcutter every time he counted his pearls he found he had more than before? You wouldn't cure him of wealth, if greed were illness, by drinking his pearls.

Whenever Finn, as now, went off to battle the Old Enemy, his monks would start to tell each other dirty jokes and scribble rude drawings. The woodcutter hoped no monk would do a dirty thing with the witch. As things stood, he was now skeptical of the dry and dusty road, but what he had failed to appreciate, was that what is safe is tedious. Success on the dry and dusty road is slow albeit certain. The big drawback of the dry and dusty road, is that men only live a certain time, and their consciousness is diminished by the fact they sleep so much. None of these monks had made much progress on the dry and dusty road, true, but a saint who achieves his sainthood on that road never loses sight of the Truth, whereas a saint who achieves his sainthood on the dark and stormy road is in constant threat of being again reduced to the level of an ass. There are many, many dark and stormy roads, half a dozen dry and dusty ones, but only one sure, safe and immediate method of finding the Truth, and that is never to have lost it in the first place. Carnal ignorance, the bright and sunny road, is, however, just for boys, and furthermore, it is given of God, so we don't go out in search of it.

'Why don't we grab him,' said a monk, 'and take him into our company? He could make a fine monk and that way, we'll gain merit in healing a future king.'

'Finn says no one is to touch him,' said the monk with the mullet, whose name was Bran. 'We have more need of him, says Finn, than he has need of us. He is a maiden, one of the one hundred and forty-four thousand undefiled of women who, when the Lamb stands on mount Sion, have the Father's name upon their forehead. Unless we too are found with that seal on our forehead upon resurrection, we shall not sing before the throne of God and the four beasts and the elders.'

'What's Finn doing there?' said the woodcutter,

all this having gone over his head. 'I have to be going shortly. Much as I've enjoyed your company, I've got to get back to my clachan. Furthermore, for your information, that child is my adopted son and I shall take him with me when I leave. He'll be too busy to do the devil's work, cutting wood for me.'

'You'd better move fast then,' said a monk, 'for there he goes. Yes he's off.'

Galahad was indeed scampering over the clearing, running like a hound and the calf after him. It happened while the woodcutter was taking leave of the monks. There was Finn, doing battle in the river, lips moving in prayer, and there was the wild, tiny child, running like a hound over the grass. Before the woodcutter had a chance to move, the boy had disappeared, and there was the calf, standing on the clearing's edge, looking back at the cow.

'He won't get far,' shouted the woodcutter, setting out in hot pursuit. 'I know this forest. I'll have him back here, soon as you like, but we may go straight to my hut. Cheerio, it's been a pleasure, and thanks again for the bannock, lads. Delicious. Give my regards to the saint and tell him I haven't forgotten how he saved my life.'

The cow imagined the woodcutter was running towards her calf, so she got upset and put a crumpled horn in the woodcutter's cape. The monks roared laughing at this, and the woodcutter grew so embarrassed he got up from where he'd been tossed and walked quickly on, without so much as a backward glance. Later, inspecting his cape well out of sight of those wretched monks, he saw the cow had ruined the one item of value he possessed. This made him all that more determined to find Galahad.

All that evening and all that night he searched for the boy, to no avail. Once he thought he heard the tiny bell-ring of a laugh, but he never saw the child, although he searched both far and wide. At dawn, bruised, defeated and still smarting over the hole in his cape, he took a final glance at the clearing just to see if the boy was there. He wasn't, but Finn, as it so happened, had emerged from his night-long vigil, and was settling down, dripping wet, to talk to his monks about what God had said. He smelt, as a Celtic saint should always smell, of attar of oak.

The woodcutter wondered what Finn would have to say, so he strolled over and sat next to the monks. The cow was bellowing, calling Galahad to breakfast.

'Fellow warriors in spiritual warfare,' declared Finn, 'hear now the Lord's Word. The Lord is righteous in all His ways and holy in all His works. We shall continue to celebrate Easter on the Sunday between the fourteenth and the twenty-second day of the moon, following John the Evangelist and Polycarp, who taught that Easter is the fourteenth day of the moon, if that day be a Sunday. We shall *never* shave the crowns of our heads behind the tips of our ears. We shall drink beer and beer only, co-warriors in spiritual warfare, for beer is our sacrament. Beer is the blood of our Saviour. Beer, fresh and effervescent as the promise of Salvation. Beer, made from the living waters that flow across this kingdom, and the corn that grows where trees were cleared to allow for the growing of corn.'

'Alleluia,' shouted the monks, as they hated the taste of red wine. 'Hooray,' shouted the woodcutter, as the saint was endorsing his vocation.

'I went to Rome once, co-warriors. It is a habitation of devils and the hold of every foul spirit and a cage of every unclean bird. All the houses are built atop each other in Rome. The Pope wears gold and precious stones and pearls. The monks don't know how to sing. It is horribly hot in summer.'

'We're not going to Rome then, Father.'

'No. But we cannot return to a monastery if it means drinking red wine. Not if it means presuming a ring of hair makes a crown of thorns. Not if it means celebrating Easter between the fifteenth and the twenty-first day of the moon.'

'Where shall we go then, Father?'

'We shall go as far from the Rule of Benedict as we can. We shall go to a desert.'

The monks sat quietly. All they could hear was the burble of the running water in the river, the rumble of a distant thundercloud, the cooing of the wood doves in the forest, and the fluttering of some little moths over some late heather flowers.

'Do we set sail, do we, Father, in search of a

desert? For we have no deserts here.'

'What is a desert?' inquired Finn. 'Does any co-warrior know?'

Bran put up a hand.

'Yes Bran?'

'A place where there's no water, Father. A place both dusty and dry. A place like the Sinai in the Holy Land of Jesus Christ Our Lord.'

'A good answer, though not the whole truth. All men have access to a desert, for a desert is a place where men can ignore the call of the Promised Land, in order to achieve resurrection as one of the one hundred and forty-four thousand to be saved when the Last Trump sounds. We cannot do that here. The Promised Land is too crowded with women, ogres, and villains. We shall have to find a desert in which to continue our war on He Who Mocks at All Good Things.'

Various monks proposed a variety of fastnesses, among them offshore islands, but these were occupied, it appeared, by agents of the Holy See.

'What about the islet in the middle of the lake where the women live under the water?'

'There's a hermit on it.'

'We could go to the middle of the forest, Father. No one would find us there.'

'How could we live in the middle of the forest? Where would we grow corn for beer? How could we stop the ogres from stealing our sacred books? Don't be stupid, Findlug. I mean to establish a monastery where monks eat at the same table, but each will have his own cell, there to wage warfare from compline to the rising bell. A desert is not a place where there is no chance of waging war. No, it is a place where spiritual life is made more easy through mortification. God, in His river, spoke to me of a fairy isle on the Edge of the World, that is not visible to humankind save once in a millennium. On a certain day in a millennium, should a man emerge from the forest, he sees before him an apparition of a village of wooden huts. And should that man be clean of sin, he sees, offshore, a fairy isle. And if a fairy boat can be found and a fairy man to row it, who's to say that mortal man could not set foot on Innisfinn? For that, I'm told, is to be the name of the isle. I'm also told that when a mortal man sets foot on Fairyland, a spell is broken.'

Here Finn stared at the woodcutter and the woodcutter stared back. You cannot get to a Fairyland on the dry and dusty road.

The
DARK
and
STORMY
Road

T HE WOODCUTTER SET out again for his clachan as the monks sang at prime, in unison, in their beautiful plainsong, 'I will bless the Lord at all times: his praise shall continually be in my mouth', and antiphonally, 'Why standest thou afar off, O Lord? Why hidest thou thyself in times of trouble?' All this for a good hour. They had fully eighty hours of hymns and psalms to be learned by rote, in the strange language they'd invented that none but they could understand. The woodcutter wasn't one for singing, although he did enjoy birdsong: the trill of the whaup, the chatter of the seapie, the kittiwake's calling its own name.

In winter, gales blew daily over these hills. A husbandman had soon to kill a calf and a dozen sheep and salt the meat. He needed to make six stones of cheese, at least, and collect a few eggs off the cliff. He needed to buy a few barrels of fish and to harvest what was left of his bere to make barley meal. The women only left their huts in winter to fetch in wood, but parliament met as usual, for the men had nothing else to do but stand about in the wind and the rain, singing the praises of the king's daughter. Once in a while, if weather permitted, the woodcutter went to the forest, but the galeforce winds made walking hard in winter.

A cascade pulsed from a hill near the sea like an arterial wound. A gale was tearing scum from a burn and translocating a waterfall. A few over-wintering blackbacked gulls, dejected and subdued, stood by the sea where low tide had exposed a metre of dulse, the texture of heather. Limpets were here for the taking, but no one bothered to glean limpets.

The woodcutter wasted no more time searching for the boy. Galahad would have to fend for himself. As soon as the king's steward saw the child he would recognize him as the king's son, and the boy would then be at the king's mercy and likely destined for execution. Well, it would be his own fault. Had not the woodcutter offered the child lodging and apprenticeship? If Galahad preferred to scamper about in the woods, that would be his folly. There's only so much a man of goodwill can do, in a world where no one takes advice.

The woodcutter walked to where he could see his clachan in the distance. Straining his eyes, he could make out parliament in session in the clachan street. The parliamentarians were all bare-headed and bare-chested and wore only the plaid, with their naked shoulders and chests and limbs camouflaged with fur, red or black. These were the woodcutter's kinsmen, bearing the same surname as himself.

The sun emerged, to illuminate the whitecaps on the grey-mauve sea, as the woodcutter suddenly realized the extent of his own disgrace. Mocked by a saint! Yet who had been the first mortal, in a thousand years, to enter Fairyland? The woodcutter. Why could no one treat him with appropriate respect? Why could he not respect himself? A woodcutter was as capable as a saint of staying up all night, and many's the time he had worked all day, and for days on end, in pouring rain, stacking wood so wet it weighed ten times its own dry weight. He was a wonderful fellow. Why could the world not see it? One of the monks, Findlug or Bran, had asked him to join the monastery, but the woodcutter had no ambitions to draw neat drawings on calf skins, when not singing psalms by the great King David seven times a day. That life held no appeal. All the woodcutter wanted was a normal life, the kind that keeps you so busy you don't have time to brood, the kind that men suppose they want until they actually achieve it. If the woodcutter could persuade his wife he regretted his recent behaviour, he hoped that all could be as it had been before he'd gone looking for the key to the door.

So he ran off, heading for the clachan and as he ran, he thought of his poor wife. Compelled to marry another! But when he thought a bit harder about this, he stopped running and began to walk.

His head started to swim. He felt suddenly faint. It couldn't be true! He hadn't really thought the thing through, you see, and now he had, he wished he hadn't. 'Not my wife,' he thought. 'Oh no, she couldn't do that. She *wouldn't* do it. She wouldn't do a dirty thing with anyone but me.'

He wasn't far from his clachan when a brother came by, dragging a pony. The woodcutter, clutching at his heart, made such a dreadful sight in the last light of day, his face a pallid mask of disbelief, his body trembling like a bridegroom's, that the brother let go the pony and ran as fast as he could towards the clachan, shouting as how he had seen the woodcutter's ghost and calling men to arms. Whereupon parliament came running out of their huts with studded clubs, and despite the woodcutter's protestations, his own beloved hounds drove him off, as his brothers dealt with him as they dealt with any troubled spirit who didn't know it was dead. They battered and bashed him. And one of the men emerged from the hut in which the woodcutter had lived.

So it was true. His wife *was* doing a dirty thing with a man who was not the woodcutter himself.

An image of the king's daughter Veronica suddenly appeared, her laugh now fully restored to its former insouciance.

'You were not meant to be my wife,' exclaimed the woodcutter. 'In fact, I can tell you were meant to be both my mother and the mother of my rivals!'

As he crawled towards her, she seemed less substantial than when he'd released her from the tower. Indeed, he could see right through her. Then she ran off, laughing, in her black gown, too fast for him to chase.

Soon after, the woodcutter lost consciousness completely. He might have lost his life, to become that restless spirit the clachan dreaded, had he not met that night with some unexpected good fortune. A tiny pair of hands grabbed his bloodied feet, another tiny pair of hands grabbed his broad shoulders, while a third tiny pair of hands grabbed his blood-matted hair. He was a big man, so there was no lifting him, but, luckily, leprechauns in those parts understood the fulcrum and the pulley, and by using tiny levers and pulleys of oak and yew, they contrived to roll him along, inadvertently staunching most of his wounds in the filthy mud. This likely saved his life, as he was bleeding very fiercely. Eventually, the leprechauns had him outside the door to their collective.

'Who's going to open the shop door?' demanded one.

'You're not!' said a second, hitting the first over the head. Leprechauns are evil-tempered elves at the best of times, but they grow exceptionally surly when forced to do hard labour. Had not Galahad appeared, war could have broken out, for it doesn't take much to upset an elf, and they never forget or forgive.

'What are you doing?' asked Galahad, knowing very well what they were doing. He could have added, so the woodcutter thought, 'Quarrelsome little creatures! You go back to your workshop at once. There'll be no human body for you to drag down to your shop tonight, lads. In fact, I was just now talking with some fairies, who were all waiting for shoes. You wasted the night you could have spent making those shoes. Now be off with you!'

The leprechauns were never clear in their minds what they meant to do with human bodies, but they generally tried experiments on them, in order to see how they worked. Unfortunately, these experiments tended to go badly, because of their great clumsiness. No matter how often they pulled off limbs they could never reattach them properly, and this, of course, only made them more ill-tempered than ever.

'Mind your own business,' said the leprechaun who'd been hit by the other. 'We heard there was a ghost in the forest so we're hauling him down to take a better look.'

'But this is not a ghost. See? There's blood coming from the nose. A ghost is a spirit with no body.'

'It is not! It's a body with no spirit!'

Well, the leprechauns were in so bad a mood there was no point arguing with them, so Galahad turned politely aside as they disappeared under a tree trunk.

Leprechauns have the notion human beings don't know where they live, and it's best not to disabuse them, as they fly in a temper on hearing any truth.

Perhaps Galahad should have gone off to fetch help, but he did nothing of the kind. He saw no problem to be resolved, for there are no problems on the bright and sunny road. Everything is just as it should be, on the bright and sunny road. There are no ambitions to be achieved, there are no scores to be settled, and no assistance may be expected from a traveller on the bright and sunny road. Because that road is no road at all and there can be no traveller upon it. In short, Galahad ran off, with a skip and a laugh, leaving the woodcutter in misery. If you need assistance on the dark and stormy road, best find yourself a friend upon the dry and dusty one.

On regaining consciousness, the woodcutter began dragging himself along the forest floor. It happened to be Halloween Eve, and young folk were bringing cattle back from the booleys. Not infrequently, a mob of cattle saw a way to escape, and in consequence, the woods were filled with the thunder of hooves and the voices of pursuers. Small black cattle were native to the Promised Land while deer were introduced, but the woodcutter knew he was dealing with domestic cattle, without opening his eyes. He was a cattleman, after all. He certainly hoped he wouldn't be trampled to death.

Late afternoon, a group came past that paused close by for a breather. They failed to notice the woodcutter, sore wounded, in the ferns.

'We lost them,' said a voice the woodcutter thought he recognized. 'What shall we do now?'

'It's getting late,' said another voice the woodcutter thought he recognized. 'I say we go back home and look for the cattle another day.'

'I agree,' said a third voice.

It was the woodcutter's own family. The third voice belonged to his seventh son, the one for whom he'd held such high hopes, but while the boy could beat a fine tattoo on any piece of goatskin, when it came to work about the place he wanted nothing to do with it.

The woodcutter thought he might lie quietly and hear what his children had to say.

'Did you bring the whistle?' said a daughter.

'I think I lost it in the chase,' came the reply, 'but it won't take me long to make another. It will give me something to do all winter, as I sit around the hearth night and day.'

At other times they avoided the hut, but in winter they sat around the hearth night and day.

'I wish we didn't have to go home, for much as I detested father, the cruel, selfish, drunken beast, he did put food on the table. He always had wood in the cleit. I don't know what this new little man will be like, in that regard.'

'He's fine! Mother loves him, that's the main concern. Why, she loves him dearly. I never saw her more happy. I'm very pleased for her. She's had that much to put up with. I think it's wonderful she meets this fellow who, first thing he does, gets rid of the roosters.'

'You think this little man will be sorry we lost his cattle?'

'Not a bit of it! Why, he cares nothing for material possessions. I never saw him lose his temper. It's true we haven't lived with him yet, but I don't expect any trouble.'

'He doesn't drink beer. I won't miss those dreadful nights, with father drinking in the corner.'

'What happened to father, do you think?'

'Who cares? Here he was, with every one of his children gifted musicians, and all he could see was lazy lumps, for he had no ear for the music.'

'Why was that, do you suppose?'

'The effects of the sound of the axe on the ear. The effects of beer on the brain.'

'There's a man lying there. Look.'

'What?'

'There.'

'That's never a man. That's a muddy tree trunk covered in moss.'

'No, it's a man. See? There's the head. There's the bum. That's an arm.'

'My God. You know who it is? Speak of the devil and he appears.'

'It's not father?'

'I wonder if he heard. If so, best kill him. That would be safest.'

'He's dead.'

'No he's not. He's unconscious. See?'

'He's pretending to be asleep.'

'What shall we do? We can't take him home.'

'Let's put him out of his misery. If he was a dog, we'd kill him.'

'You can't kill your own father!'

'He would have been snooping about the booley. It must have been him took those lambs.'

'I have a problem. See, I assumed he was dead when I split the estate.'

'Wake him. Go on! Hit him over the head. Harder!'

'Let's think it through. There's not much chance he'll live to bother us. I don't think we need to kill him. Let's just leave him where he is.'

'Why don't we take him back to the clearing? You know, the clearing where we saw the monks? Then it would be their fault if he dies.'

'That's a great idea.'

'He must have known what happened in the clachan. I'll bet he's been prowling round, spying on mother. He probably steals a bit of corn.'

'Has no one a good thing to say for the man? I mean, for all his faults, he *is* our father.'

'If he is our father, I don't know where we get our tastes in music. If only he could have let us play our instruments in the hut.'

Now the woodcutter, never opening his eyes,

wondered if this were a nightmare. Eventually he passed out, and woke up later that day on the edge of the clearing. Yes, it was the clearing where he'd met the monks. But as it turned out, the monks had gone off to the Edge of the World to look around.

Next day at noon the rain stopped, for a bit, and the witch appeared in a short dress.

'What happened to you?' she said. 'Why, look at all your cuts and scratches!'

She went to fetch herbs. Puffballs to staunch his wounds, henbane for his toothache. The cow stood ruminating by the calf. There was no sign of the feral boy.

The woodcutter wondered, as often he had, if he'd been killed when the witch pulled him open. Perhaps he was indeed that ghost his brothers took him to be.

Ghost or not, she patched him up, her arms all over his body. But you can't feel jealous of a girl who would do a dirty thing with any man. She can be as good company as a girl who would never do a dirty thing.

'I can't go back to my hut,' he complained. 'Would you like me to tell you why?'

'No, I want you to rest now. Come on. You get some sleep.'

But the woodcutter couldn't sleep. He had scarcely slept or eaten in days.

The witch sat him up against the stump of the oak in the middle of the clearing. He noticed a henge he hadn't seen before, with all the standing stones fallen.

The cow was pulling on what grass there was, but there wasn't much grass about. With no trees to keep the rain off the ground, the minerals had leached through the soil to form an impervious iron pan a metre or so below the surface, and this pan had caused big pools of water to lie about when it rained. And it rained all the time. Moss and sedges grew in the mud to build an acid environment, which encouraged the growth of more mosses and sedges and rotted slowly to build a bog on which nothing would grow except heather. Why, this meadow was being ruined because of the dark and stormy weather!

'What can we do about the weather?' said the woodcutter. The witch didn't know. She didn't want to talk about the king's daughter, either, to the woodcutter's chagrin.

'I don't believe in the king's daughter,' she said. 'I don't believe in fairies. I don't believe in ogres. I don't believe in devils. I don't believe in elves. I believe in *this*!' And she rapped the stump. Then she put a question to him.

'Did you cut down this tree?'

'Me? I never cut down a central tree I leave standing in a meadow. If you want my opinion, it's someone else cutting down these trees. I don't approve of it.'

'You destroyed the forest with your iron axe.'

'Oh don't let me hear that kind of talk! You'll upset me, and I'm too ill to be upset. Let's not go on about it.

There are millions and millions of oak trees left reproducing from acorns. Let's change the subject. I hear you're in the king's pay. Is it true you know the king?'

'The king is a poor, sick man.'

'Now how can you call him a poor, sick man when he's rich and famous and has lived so very long?'

'What hope for our Promised Land that is all full of these Christians? They want a city paved with gold. And I suppose you're a Christian?'

'I have my own ideas,' said the woodcutter, 'though I can't say I was ever in a church, and I was never baptized or shriven, but yes, I would call myself a Christian of a kind. I have a bad conscience over certain matters. If you wear a crucifix it acts as a breastplate to protect you from your conscience. That, I know for a fact. It keeps you safe from women and ogres. It protected me from you.'

'Women and ogres. You see, that's what I can't stand about the king, he's made men so afraid of women. And because men are so afraid of women they cultivate illusion. They construct fictions. Because they don't want to compete.'

'What do you mean "compete"? Show me a man who could match me in a feat of strength on any day but this!'

'You need more than strength to father my child but no man competes wholeheartedly. For which, I blame the Christians. But you are *meant* to compete. You are *built* to compete! Where's that … '

'Hey! What are you doing?'

'Ha. Got it. Why is it shaped like this?'

She had pulled out the dirty thing from between his legs and was inspecting it.

'I'll tell you. Because it is a plunger built to break a soft plug. Now a soft plug of what? It is built to undo what is already done, the filthiness of fornications. But where does that leave a faithful wife?'

'Help! Christians to the rescue!'

'It's getting bigger now. Big enough soon to remove a soft plug? I'll tell you what your round tower is for. It is built to destroy the treachery of women. So why not accept that treachery? Why object to our natures? Why not accept that men and women alike have treachery inbuilt? *Your* treachery makes a whore of every faithful wife! If only the king could find the key to his tower, all would be well. This lover of yours, has she a body? This fairy woman you're enamoured of?'

'Sometimes.'

'Sometimes, he says. And does she do wees and poos?'

'I doubt that.'

'Oh, you doubt that. And has she a dirty thing between her legs?'

'Absolutely not!'

'Then she would have no use for this. How could she be a mother? How can she be a wife? That's why your king has no mother and no wife. Get away with you now.'

'I'm too ill to move!'

'Suit yourself. But if you're still here when I finish this wees and poos I'm about to commence, we'll be doing a dirty thing together, you and I.'

The poor woodcutter had no choice but to crawl off, bleeding, into the oak.

Often, when ill with microbes, he'd wanted to give away all he owned and now, as the fever consumed him, he felt the impulse again. But having lost his otter-fur cape, he had nothing left to give.

He crawled clean through that forest and out the other side. He covered quite a bit of ground that day. Evening found him sitting on a salt-soaked promontory of sea-pink and bucks-horn plantain, the sea roaring before him and the forest roaring behind. It was dark and particularly stormy.

'I might jump off a cliff,' he thought, 'and put myself out of misery. I've obviously got the plague. I must have caught it from the boy's mother. That's what you get for lending people clothes.' He could hear the whoosh and kthunk of the waves as they broke against the cliff face, coming in in their sets of four to six with a lull between.

'Thank you,' he whispered in a voice that, when he felt himself in trouble, rose from bass to alto. He was thanking his mother for the life that he had led, which had had pleasant moments. Strange how he seemed to know a fairy woman better than he knew his own wives.

But to his surprise, Veronica's image did not appear, as he gave thanks. He was not thinking of his own mother, nor was he thinking of his own wife.

The pain in his leg disappeared. He reached down his hand to check. He felt himself cooling down.

'Must I go on?' he said to himself. 'Very well then, I shall!'

A thought occurred: if he were just one person, how come he talked so fluently to himself?

The commonest flowers on the Edge of the World were thyme, milkwort, ragged robin – pink, pale blue, violet. The hills where trees had been cleared away were heather, stunted bracken, spongy sphagnum moss. The Edge of the World was a jungle of lichen, arctic rain-forest, dyer's paradise, and in the winter the colour came from the lichen on the rocks – white, chocolate, lime green, sulphur, gunmetal grey, every tint of ochre. The woodcutter wandered along the shore, picking up bits of grey driftwood. The beaches here were littered with limbs from far-off virgin forests, and the woodcutter saw these as a vindication of his calling. He stopped to pick up a cod that had stranded itself in a rock pool, then bit off the head and cooked it over a fire he had lit from the driftwood he had gathered.

'I must look like a caveman,' he thought, glancing down at his body with a laugh. In lieu of plaid he was wearing a pussycat skin he'd found on the beach. Poor old cavemen! They hadn't known where to begin in dealing with the oak. Pine and alder they'd managed to burn, but slogging away with a stone axe wouldn't get you far with oak trees. The poor beggars had ended up on the beaches, eating limpets.

A couple of monks appeared. They wandered up from the beach as soon as they saw the woodcutter's fire. Soaked in spray, they were no doubt very pleased to see a fire burning.

'Findlug and Bran isn't it? Where you off to, lads?'

'We're looking for that fairy isle,' said Bran, 'but we don't know where to start.'

'You should have asked me,' said the woodcutter. '*I*'d have known where to start.'

Bran took out a line and threw it in the sea, fishing for saithe. He had, the woodcutter noticed, bait on his hook in contravention of the saint's edict.

'We're not happy,' admitted Findlug. 'We don't think the island exists.'

'And what about Finn?' said the woodcutter. 'What does your saint have to say?'

'He says it's there. He thinks it's close by. It's the will of God, according to him, that we go there and nowhere else. So we're not happy.'

In contrast, the woodcutter's face had broken out in a broad grin. It was so long since he had grinned, his poor lips cracked wide open.

'I've nothing on at present,' he said. 'Would you like me to show you the isle?'

The

BRIGHT

and

SUNNY

Road

T HE MONKS, WITH the saint, were singing, for sext, in unison, 'The earth is the Lord's and the fullness thereof; the world, and they that dwell therein', and, antiphonally, 'I waited patiently for the Lord; and he inclined unto me and heard my cry. He brought me up also out of an horrible pit, out of the miry clay, and set my feet upon a rock.' All this, in the strange language they'd invented that none but they could understand.

'Follow me!' said the woodcutter. 'I'll show you the desert you seek, for certain it is, I was there. I am the man who, coming from the forest, saw before him the village of wooden huts. But only six monks can come. There's room on the isle for no more than six beehive huts and one oratory.'

'What a pity,' said Finn, 'for we boast here a fine choir of voices. We often sing our Songs of Degrees from matins through to compline, as we aspire towards hermitage. True hermits don't work but only sing the Lord's praise, and such food as they eat must fall in their laps or else they starve.'

'What a lazy lot,' said the woodcutter, 'pardon me if I say so. It would do no harm for all to row, I suppose, but half may not survive.'

'Show us where you saw this Fairyland,' insisted Finn.

The sinner chosen by God led the saint along the shore of benthic shells until they came to a marvellous sight together. A section of sandy shore, tied with a pubic knot of marram grass, had covered itself in a superabundance of flowers, notwithstanding the season. There was pink fumitory, violet hemp nettles, yellow archangel, silverweed, sorrel, and in their midst, to clinch the matter for the sinner, a cord of oak wood.

'This is the place,' declared the woodcutter, 'as we see by this miracle.'

'Can you see the fairy isle?' insisted Finn.

'No. Not since I lost my key to the door, I can't see it.'

'Then what use are you? I best pray.' Finn went to pray in the sea. Two sea otters came alongside him and kept him warm as he prayed.

The woodcutter, meanwhile, went to check the cord of oak, having sent the monks to fetch driftwood.

He acted as the leading hand and gave orders when the saint was doing battle. Most of these monks were just boys and happy to take orders. They had dodged their responsibilities, according to the woodcutter's wife, who had no time for the Christian religion, seeing it, rightly, as a threat to matrimony.

The wood was green. The wood was fresh. It was still red on the inside and some of the cuts had bark attached. The woodcutter counted the rings in the wood. He saw that all this wood had come from the one tree, and what an axeman! With what precision the cuts had been made! Why, it was as though the whole tree had been felled with a single blow. Beneath each cut, on the bark, could be seen a row of tiny teeth, as though a pussycat had held the trunk in its mouth.

There was but one conclusion to be drawn. A giant was roaming the woodcutter's meadows, falling the trees that remained. And these were the very trees spared by the woodcutter, to provide shade.

What was worse, the giant could appear from the forest at any moment and the woodcutter knew he would have to attack him, if only to commandeer the axe.

'Bran,' said the woodcutter, 'do you know how to build a currach?'

'I helped build a coracle once.'

'We might build a currach. Or we could hollow out an oak log. We don't want sail. Too much trouble.'

'We need iron tools.'

'That's true.'

The woodcutter knew how to smelt ore. He could certainly build a nail, but he wasn't sure he had the skills, leave alone the ore, to build an axe. With iron tools, the monks could improvise ribs and a frame, then stretch a tanned ox-hide over oak bark to fashion a waterproof skin. Alternatively, they could hollow out a log of oak. But they would need an iron axe.

'My mother has an iron axe. It belonged to my father who was never a woodcutter. He wouldn't leave that axe to me. We lived there.' And the woodcutter pointed towards the scrubland at the far end of the kingdom, where willows, birch and hazel grew, with a few wild berries and herbs.

'Why not visit your mother?' said Bran.

'She might not like it I have a new mother, better than herself.'

'Go see her in any event,' said Bran. 'We need the axe.'

'All right. Tell the saint I'm gone, but don't tell him where I'm going.'

With that, the woodcutter set off again, leaving the scholar on the beach.

Instinctively, he moved back into the forest when it grew dark, because he found the sand too cold and wet to sleep upon. He was lying quietly, looking up at the stars and wishing he could sleep, when the leprechaun appeared.

'You again!' said the leprechaun. 'Haven't you a home to go to?'

'I don't,' admitted the woodcutter, 'and I thank you for that. Now please don't ask me again if I mean to cut down these trees. I would if I could, but I've lost my axe. See? I no longer have an axe.'

'I hear tell,' said the leprechaun, drawing close, 'that the woodcutter's got out of gaol. Is that true?'

'You mean me?'

'No! I mean the giant who screams and roars as he cuts down trees. My god, he's cut some trees down. All the big trees in each meadow.'

'And what does your ogre have to say?'

'Our ogre has nothing to say. The screaming comes only from cleared meadows where ogres never venture.'

'*I* was the woodcutter cleared those meadows! That wood was properly mine. Now listen: regarding this Land where Stories End. Is it a Fairyland?'

'It is.'

'And could I take a party of monks out there to build a monastery?'

The leprechaun laughed till his face became as red as his Phrygian hat. He slapped his stonewashed jeans.

'That's a joke,' he said, 'a monastery on a Fairyland! That would be a sight to see.'

'Why's that?'

'Because Fairyland is no place for a monk! Fairies come to your land but you can't go to theirs. Anyway, you won't find Fairyland. You lost your key to the door to the tower and that was your key to that land. Without that key, you've no way to find Fairyland again. It won't appear to you.'

'But what if I set my foot on Fairyland. What would happen then?'

'If you were there to be married, I suppose it would have to appear, but not to you. Only a man clean of sin can see the Land where Stories End and you, my friend, have become a great sinner, in recent times. But no mortal remains long. Some two hours, some four, but none longer than a day, although a day in the Land where Stories End would seem an Eternity. That is because Fairyland is a spiritual place and you are not a spirit.'

'That's a relief. My brothers had their doubts.'

The leprechaun laughed. 'I'll teach you how to tell the difference,' he said, 'although I know I shouldn't. Saints and sinners do wees and poos but fairies don't. Now you didn't hear me say it.'

As per usual, he disappeared. Suddenly, as he always did.

'What was that about,' thought the woodcutter. At first light, hearing screaming from a meadow, he ran off as quickly as he could.

The woodcutter's mother lived on the sandy soil in a stalled cairn, a small village made of flagstones built inside a rubbish heap, with interconnecting passageways between the several stalls. The rubbish, which had been allowed to ripen, consisted of wees and poos, inter-mixed with stones and shells and broken animal bones and guts. Because of its age it didn't smell, which was as well, as the stalls were covered in it.

The woodcutter couldn't recall the last time he'd visited his childhood home, although he did remember mending a stall a storm had half-destroyed. His father, together with his father's brothers, had quarried sand-stone from a nearby cliff, then broken it to flags by first splitting it with wooden wedges, then heating it over a fire. There were dwarf willows growing by the burn into which they tossed the stones to cool and split, but noth-ing, on these sandy soils, was of much interest to a woodcutter. As soon as he'd learned to throw an axe, the woodcutter had gone to live near the oak, as had his brothers and neighbours. Then sea raiders, according to rumour, had taken the remaining children, murdered the remaining men, and married the remaining girls, but the old women, being deemed of no use to anyone, had been ignored. Over the years they'd died off, leav-ing only the woodcutter's mother. At seven times ten, she was probably the oldest woman in the whole Promised Land. She had no teeth. You could tell how very old she was from the dung heap she'd constructed. It was already big enough to contain a cairn of four stalls.

Nowadays, no one wanted to live quite so close to the neighbours. The stalled cairn had vanished elsewhere during the late Stone Age, but fashion moved more slowly here in the kingdom on the World's Edge. In a stalled cairn, the rooms were only a metre or two apart, and all were under the same turfed roof of wees and poos turned clay. The cairn certainly kept out wind and dogs more effectively than a village of huts, but when you did a dirty thing in a cairn everyone could hear, and if you were drunk, you'd often enter the wrong stall by mistake. They were all very much the same.

The woodcutter took a quick look about the workshop, before crawling down the main passage. He could see there'd been no fire lit in the workshop hearth for years, and he found no tools in the stone dresser, only cherts and flints. Selecting one or two of the sharper flints he thrust these in his beard, then, having adjusted his pussycat skin so as to cover his bum, he called out for his mother in his boldest, loudest voice. He didn't really think she could be still alive.

'Why won't you answer the door when I call your name? Silly old fool!'

These were the first words the woodcutter said to his mother after all those years. He'd had to spend the rest of the day pulling doors off stalls, as someone had barred them up, using whalebone bars. It was a dreadful job. The doors opened out into the cramped passageways, but the passages were blocked, and no sooner had the woodcutter dug out the sand than the wind blew it all back in. So he was in a filthy mood by the time he came upon his poor mother who, wouldn't you know it, had hidden herself in the last stall of the cairn. It wasn't actually her stall but she had the run of the place.

She was wearing what had once been a white cloth over her head and what had once been a white cloak held with a broach. 'Is anyone about?' she asked.

'Is that all you can say? Here's a son pays a visit after God knows how long and all you can ask, is anyone about. Don't you want to know if I succeeded in life? What's this you have burning here. Phoor! Poo! Can't you find a whalebone to burn? Haven't you a lamp to see by? Why does your limpet box leak?'

A man who has glimpsed the Land where Stories End becomes worse-tempered than before.

'Was anyone about, son?'

'No one was about. I didn't come by sea, if you must know. I came by land. I didn't see anyone. No one comes here.'

'I wouldn't like you to say that to Coll.'

'Coll?'

'I wouldn't want Coll to know. Now tell me, is anyone about?'

He could tell this would not be easy. Reassuring her that no one was about and that he wouldn't tell Coll, the woodcutter walked across the flagstone floor to check the limpet boxes. Each stall had two or three flagstone boxes, the joints luted with dried poo, and in these boxes limpets had been softened, in former days, to make fish bait. The woodcutter knew, from the smell, that his mother had been eating limpets herself. It appeared she lived by gathering limpets and possibly hazelnuts.

'Let me see you,' said his mother, as he set about mending the box, which was oozing water over the floor and wetting the central hearth. He doubted she could see him, as her eyes were white and opaque as two shells.

'Sorry I didn't visit,' he said, without a great deal of contrition. 'I've had a lot on and wasn't sure you'd be here. You must be a great age.'

'You were taken,' said his mother, after a bit. 'I see it in your face. Don't tell Coll, for I won't have Coll upset.'

'What do you mean "taken" mother? Taken by what? Taken by whom? I'll have to get something to mend this box. You wouldn't have an iron axe? Look, there's limpets all over the floor. It's like a rock shelf, this stall of yours. What have you done with the iron tools? Where's father's iron axe?'

'You were taken by fairies. I see it in your face. Whenever a mortal man is taken by fairies it shows in his face.'

'But bear in mind it's a long time since we met and the years take a toll.'

'It's not the years took this toll. Oh no, I see you lost your teeth and you always were an ugly lad, but no, it's the grief in your eyes, boy. You've seen a world you never should have and now you long to return. Am I wrong? I saw that look in the face of a girl who was taken in childbirth, poor lass. Is anyone about, son?'

'No one's about. Did this lass say what she'd seen?'

'She tried, but no one could understand her, so she stopped. It vexed her, but don't tell Coll.'

'Who's Coll, mother?'

'Coll is my newfound suffering son and I am Coll's sorrowing mother. Oh, he's the finest son a woman could have. He attends my every need. I can't see him, which is to the good, but I know he's with me night and day. I'm always talking to him. He dies on the darkest day each winter, and that's when I give him birth. Oh, he's a bonny little bairn. Coll shows me where limpets cling. I don't think he'd like you being here.'

'Don't worry. Tell him I'm off, as soon as I find the iron tools. I'm building a boat, for to take me back to Fairyland, with a few lads.'

'I knew you'd been to Fairyland. What did you like best about the place?'

The woodcutter thought hard about this and not for the first time.

'I liked the way I was filled with love for all mankind while I was there, mother. I felt the world's pain, which became mine, as I had none left of my own. I felt a tenderness for you folk, as I could see you have it all wrong, and I was filled with the burning need to put you straight and correct your every error.'

'We wouldn't like that, son. Not from you.'

'You didn't. Because you can't and won't be helped. Well, too bad, because next time I return, I intend to confine myself to healing the king.'

'Oh stop, son! This is rubbish that you speak. I can't make head nor tail of it. It's wrong, it's arrogant, it's misguided, in fact, it's quite ridiculous. You'd be the worst-tempered man in the world and you've no love for anyone but yourself. Stop, before you're telling me you speak with leprechauns.'

'I'll fix this another time. I see you manage quite well with Coll's help. You don't need me.'

'You were never here. I heard you scream once. Did you once scream?'

'That girl of whom you spoke, mother, did she want to come back here?'

'She did not. She was ill-tempered and discontented.'

'What happened to her?'

'Sea raiders took her. She was a pretty lass. Now didn't we tell you never to speak to fairies, your father and I? Those who speak with fairies always live in a state of confusion. I sometimes think it were better for the human race were they to disappear.'

'They're disappearing. I know a girl who doesn't think they exist.'

'Well, she'll be punished for that but she won't see how and she won't know why.'

'That axe, mother. Father's axe. I need it to fix the limpet box.'

'I have it behind my dresser.'

'Right. Give it here and I'm off. You get Coll to fix your limpet box.'

He stormed off in a temper but later felt bad and came back and fixed the limpet box.

That night, hugging the axe as he lay to sleep in the forest, he felt a bit gloomy about going back to Fairyland. 'What's to be gained in having this experience I can't share with anyone?' he thought. 'Oh well, at least I'll have company next time I'm out there.'

He didn't want to share the king's daughter with those dirty-minded monks. It was bad enough his own mother expecting him to share this fairy son of hers. As he slept, the woodcutter dreamt of the girl who'd been taken by fairies. How pleased she would be to find him. How grateful she would be to meet the one man in the world who understood what she'd been through. Why, she would find him irresistible. But as he reached towards her in his dream, he woke, and saw the virtue of the dry and dusty road. He could see that his own dark and stormy road was a twisting lane, just wide enough for one, while the dry and dusty road was a straight and broad road, wide enough for the whole world.

Just then, Galahad ran by. It was a bright and sunny morning.

'Look at you, naked,' said the woodcutter. 'Why, you'll catch your death of cold. What do you eat?'

He was starting to think if he caught the child he could take him to visit the king, and the king might well reward him, for the introduction, with a bag of pearls.

'Crabapples, blackberries, hazelnuts, pine-cones, acorns,' laughed the boy, 'though I'm seldom hungry.'

'What a diet! No wonder that you're not growing as a boy should. I don't think you've grown since last we met. A growing boy needs proper food. I'll tell you what I eat. I eat horses, beef, lamb, pork, venison, goat, cod, saithe, lobsters, dogs, crabs, mussels, urchins, eels, whales, dolphins, ducks, gannets, guillemots, auks, great auks – Gotcha!'

'Let me go!'

'Ha. You're coming with me to the king's palace. I want you to meet your father. If my poor father could leave me an axe, what could your father not leave you? You could be wearing a suit of fine clothing and sitting in a well-constructed counting house, eating cheese and drinking beer.'

'I don't like beer! I don't want pearls! I've no use for a suit of clothing!'

'Hush. You're just a young lad and you don't understand this world. It's not as we would wish it. You'll change your tune as you grow, *if* you grow. For that, you need proper nourishment. You'll thank me for this some day. Come, you're going over my shoulders. That's it. I won't have argument from you. Let's be realistic. Don't worry, I don't mean to ask you to work for me again. I don't think you've the strength for it. A woodcutter needs proper food if he's cutting down trees all day. How's that witch? You know, the one with the long black hair? She's fond of me.'

'No she's not. She thinks you're stupid. She says you want things both ways and can't make up your mind.'

They reached the palace on dusk. The king was in his counting house, as usual. When the woodcutter, holding the boy on his shoulders, asked if they might speak with the king, the guard, instead of calling for an executioner, drew the woodcutter aside.

'Mate,' he said, 'I'm worried about the king. He don't seem able to repair himself. There he is, with his arms in the air, back bent, and his legs have fallen off.'

'What!'

'Both the king's legs have fallen off. I think he has the plague. You see for yourself, that's if he agrees to an audience. Don't mention the legs, unless he mentions them first.'

The woodcutter agreed to this and the king agreed to the audience, although it couldn't be held in the counting house, for security reasons. The guard went to speak to the king. He returned with the king on his shoulders. The king was just as the guard had said; head bent, neck crooked, legs disappeared and holding his arms in the air. Nonetheless, he seemed in high spirits.

'Israel!' he said. 'I hope you're here to tell me you found the key to the door. Because I lost mine.'

'Better yet,' said the woodcutter, 'I've a boy here doesn't need the key! Permit me to introduce to you your son and heir, Your Majesty.'

'Grace. That's what I call a maiden. I call him Grace. Don't mind me I'm bleeding, Grace. This is Israel, who released my daughter from the tower, but not for long.'

'That reminds me,' said the woodcutter. 'I found a saint who wants to live on the Land where Stories End.'

'Christian,' said the king. 'That's what I call a saint. If you're not a saint you're not a Christian, you're just a would-be if you could-be. Christian means well but he's a dull fellow. He won't compete but take him out to sea.'

'Does he find the key to the door?'

'Not your key to the door, no. Christian would be the last man I'd set to fetch a Philistine's foreskin, even though he's always singing psalms. Oh I wish he wouldn't do it. Let that child down now, Israel. Let him run into the forest, that's right. I don't want Grace to know what a foreskin is, let alone what it's for. He's a maiden.'

'Majesty, the blood is dripping down your nose and onto the guard's head.'

'I'm aware of it. I don't seem able to heal myself. It's because I'm king of the Promised Land and king of

Fairyland as well. It's all too much. I don't seem able to die a natural death, so I may ask you to kill me, Israel.'

'No!'

'I've too many enemies. That's my problem, wearing this dual crown. The Old Enemy of the Promised Land is within me, too small for me to see. He is, in fact, a microbe.'

'And Veronica? I ask, because she made such a mess of my life.'

'She is made in the image of the Old Enemy of Fairyland. You contain her but she does not contain you. I hope that clarifies matters. Now give my regards to Christian and good luck to you both. I must look for the key.'

'What about Grace, Your Majesty? I believe that boy is your son and heir!'

'He certainly is my son and heir but he is already happy ever after.'

There was no doubt the king was ill and quite as confused as the woodcutter. 'If the king himself can't make sense of Creation,' thought the woodcutter, 'what hope have I? After all, I'm just a poor woodcutter. He's the king of the two worlds.'

The king's palace, you may recall, was not far from the woodcutter's clachan, but the woodcutter wasn't about to return home for fear of being beaten up again. Instead, he spent an interesting hour among a

161

mob of men who were watching a man trying to open the door to the monastery tower. This man had built a battering ram of oak, which he carried on his shoulders, and of course, as soon as his second bash at the door was deemed to have failed, he was grabbed by the king's executioners, dreadful-looking fellows wearing leather vests with sharp silver studs and poo over their hands, and they took him off to be tortured and broken at the wheel, as the mob jeered.

When the mob had gone, the woodcutter went through the rubbish they'd left behind, in the hope of finding a bottle of beer that wasn't completely empty. He found a few, which cheered him up. He was just draining the last drop of beer from the last bottle he had found, and preparing to walk off down the coast, into the lightning that he could see and the thunder that he could hear, when he heard the ringing of the hand bell.

It was the king's daughter. She rang the bell a dozen times, at intervals of a second. But he was no longer sure of who she was, if she couldn't be his mother and she couldn't be his wife.

He then found a sporran of acorns, curiously pierced, by the monastery gate, and shoved about eight or a dozen of these into his beard, Heaven knows why. He then walked towards the beach from where he'd seen the Land where Stories End.

The woodcutter didn't really want the king's pearls. He'd be fighting off thieves forever. He didn't really want the king's daughter's hand. He'd be fighting off rivals forever. He didn't want to be heir to the throne, if it meant catching the plague. He just wanted to be happy ever after, and though wiser, he was no happier. 'I *will* become a monk,' he thought, 'just to see if it can make me happy.'

To his surprise, he found he still had the iron axe in his hand. He wondered if he could chop down trees, as well now as formerly. So he waited till he found a suitable meadow, then, squaring off against an oak that still stood in the middle of this meadow, struck it with the axe as hard as he could.

His body received a dreadful jarring and the acorns he held in his beard jumped out, together with a couple of flints. No sooner had the acorns hit the ground than they began to germinate. The woodcutter, tingling in his arms from the terrible jarring he had received, looked on amazed as the acorns sprouted into saplings then threw out branches. It all happened so quickly the woodcutter had no chance to escape. The saplings grew into trees so tall the woodcutter couldn't see their crowns and he had no room to squeeze out from them. They had him completely trapped. At first, he thought he would be crushed to death, but this wasn't to be, or not at first, for the instant a tree touched the woodcutter's skin, it settled into a dormancy. They left him room enough to draw breath, if no room to swing an axe.

Normally, in such a situation, he would have

screamed, 'Christians to the rescue!' but the only person who could help him now was the giant who was cutting down his trees. The woodcutter didn't want to be indebted to anyone who cut trees better than himself, and he felt he would rather die than hear that unChristian scream again.

Just then, a leprechaun appeared. It was probably the same one as usual.

'Zblood,' said the leprechaun, 'you're in a mess. I can't see you getting out of there. Did you drop a pierced acorn? You never should have picked it up.'

'Get me out,' said the woodcutter. 'I'm no ordinary man. I've been to Fairyland and back and am off to Fairyland again!'

'What would you give me to get you out? Have you any black pearls at all?'

'No, but I can get some. How many do you need?'

'An elf could never have too many pearls. How many can you get?'

'What about all the pearls in the king's counting house? How would that do?'

'How would you get the pearls from the king? Why, you're nothing but a thief! I'd rather have the daughter you make with the witch, when you do a dirty thing with her.'

'I'll not do a dirty thing with her. I mean to become a Christian monk. How would you like, instead, one of my seventeen existing children? You can have the lot.'

'No! They're all too fat and lazy. They're no good to anyone. We know you're a thief, as you stole the glimpse of Fairyland, so just steal me the king's pearls and I'll tell you how to get out.'

'Right.'

'Cut off your legs! I reckon if we cut off your legs we could get you out. Give us the axe and I'll have a swing.'

'No! You'll not cut off my handsome legs. I seem to recall there was nothing to fear in being dead, so I'm not too concerned. I'm not as desperate as you seem to think. You didn't hear me call for help!'

'Suit yourself. But once you're dead I'll cut off your legs in any event.'

'I won't care what you do to me once I'm dead.'

'That's what you think! You know, for a man who's been to Fairyland and back you haven't learned much.'

'I learned a great deal more than you realize, and while I've forgotten it again, that was only because I had responsibilities in the Promised Land. When a man has responsibilities he can't just walk away from them. Not that I expect a leprechaun knows much about responsibility.'

'We know nothing about responsibility! Why, we hardly ever do our own work. When did you last see a fairy wearing a pair of shoes?'

So saying, he disappeared.

The woodcutter knew he could live a month

without food, and water was no problem. When it didn't rain here it poured. All you had to do was open your mouth. What worried him most was the thought of being eaten alive by an animal. Had he found an animal in the predicament he was in, he would have eaten it. But animals didn't always kill you, before they ate you, that was the problem. The woodcutter, to his credit, always killed animals before he ate them, although he could never be completely certain in the case of those he ate raw and fresh. Still, he wasn't in dire straits yet, as there was no sign of the king's daughter.

The woodcutter studied the tree he could see, pressed against his own spine. It was oak, as he saw from the bark.

'There's something funny here,' he thought. 'If these trees can grow so fast, then why have they suddenly stopped? There's no movement in that trunk, yet I can't think it's fully grown as yet. Perhaps I ought to address these trees, on the offchance they can hear me. A tree that could grow as fast as these is capable of anything.'

So he started talking to the trees. He pointed out that he regretted having cut down so many, and promised he wouldn't do it again. He said the axe was just for building the boat, which is why he couldn't drop it, and needed, as well, for his personal protection, now he had lost his crucifix. If these trees had formed a wrong impression, supposing he meant to kill the tree he'd hit, let them be assured he had only meant to hit it once, to see if he could still hit well. He wanted to see if he had strength in his arm, after so long a lay-off. Why, didn't they know he meant to be a monk, who intended to go where no trees grew, unless you counted dwarf willows which no woodcutter would fall?

'I further declare,' he asserted in conclusion, 'that if you spare my life, I shall plant your speedy acorns in every meadow of the Promised Land. Even though it means undoing a life's work on my part, I won't be worried, as I'm heading for a desert, never to return.'

At once, the trees began to stir and acorns rained down like hail. As the trees resumed expanding, they crushed the voice out of the woodcutter. They added years of growth to their trunks in what seemed a split second. The woodcutter felt his head being pushed between his filthy toes and his arms wrenched from their fetid sockets, but he didn't let go of his axe. He couldn't see the king's daughter, no matter what sort of trouble he was in, because, he now realized, she couldn't be his mother and she couldn't be his wife. That had been hardly fair, he now saw, to his existing mother and his existing wife.

The oak trees crushed the woodcutter till he was no thicker than his own skin. They squashed him till he resembled a puffin, turned inside out by a greater black-backed gull. They mashed him till his tongue went black and his eyes popped out like boiled eggs, and they scrunched him till his blood went white, or pretty close to white.

He was finished. He was dying. He was dead.

And the next thing he knew the trees had died, having reached the end of their life cycles, and it was quiet, and the sun was still in the sky and the wood pigeons were still cooing, and the woodcutter looked up at his body, from between his toes, and it seemed to be all there. It seemed to be all right. He hit himself with the axe, to make sure.

It took him a while to chip himself out of that oak wood with the iron axe, because it was blunt, and his arms were in the wrong position to cut. But he was persistent.

What a relief to feel his feet back on the prickly heather! He saw on the heather about him acorns by the thousands, all dead. And growing nearby was a shrub and a tree he didn't recognize at all. The shrub had pretty little red bell flowers and the tree had shiny green leaves.

The woodcutter chopped a few big limbs from the now deceased oak, in order to incorporate the wood into the currach he meant to build with the monks.

A

DESERT

in the

OCEAN

ALL THAT WINTER they built the currach, too large, using the iron axe. The woodcutter had become a monk of a sort, though he couldn't be a real one, because these monks, including the priests among them, were hell-bound. In refusing to accept the correct date for Easter, in cutting their hair in this ridiculous manner, in drinking beer instead of wine in the sacrifice of their divine victim, they were anathema, not just to Rome, but to Byzantium. Their lives could be no example to others of what had been lost in the Promised Land. As long as they stayed out of the way, though, no one could be bothered chasing them, least of all a sick king. The woodcutter was the one convert they were ever likely to make, and when they died, the Celtic Christian Church would die as well.

The saint was as bitter as the woodcutter, on those rare occasions when he'd had a sleep and a feed. The woodcutter saw that, after he'd eaten and slept, Finn became unsaintly, and it was then they enjoyed a conversation, as they watched the other monks working on the boat. It was late winter, pouring cold rain, but they slept on the beach and ate limpets.

One morning, after Finn had slept for twenty-four hours straight and eaten ten cod, he called the woodcutter over to where he lay sprawled, propped up against a rock. Although it was winter, there was spring in the air, and it wouldn't be long before the lavy returned to the ledge. Lavy (guillemot), a small auk not much fancied as meat, has fat little wings like a seal's flippers, designed for swimming not flight. It tastes like a ten-year-old rooster pickled in sprat brine and cod-liver oil. You'd often see a lavy raft, among the common seals in a bay, but here there were no protected waters outside the harbour, only kelp-laden swell. Because of the driftwood on the beach, there was ample wood with which to build the boat, and the giant never appeared to collect his cord of fresh-cut oak.

Finn stared into a whisky.

'Let's talk of islands,' he said, patting the sand beside him where he sat. 'You say this island can be seen from shore?'

'It's only ten kilometres offshore, Father.'

'I like islands. If I weren't a saint I'm sure to have been a farmer. I wouldn't pay a rogue like you to clear my timber, though! I wouldn't pay a fellow like you.'

The woodcutter laughed, for he knew the saint enjoyed a joke when he wasn't feeling saintly. 'Sure, I'd clear your meadow just for wood,' he replied. 'You'd get pasture and we'd both be happy.'

'Don't speak to me of happiness, man! Not when I'm in the mood for a laugh. Ten kilometres, you say? Strange we can't see it. That's a good distance. Islands, where you can jump from the mainland to the island, I don't call those islands. That'd be an island a pope might call an island, but I wouldn't call that an island. An island, to be safe from attack, should be remote, yet not too far from help. You may want help on occasion. You must be able to see your island, in the distance, as the mainland recedes, but you don't want to be able to see the mainland from your island, or only as a blur. An island should be mountainous, so that you can savour it for hours at sea. Your imagination must fix upon it, in the approach and the departure. It ought to contain at least one peak from which the whole shoreline can be seen, and it ought to be small enough that you could walk around it in a single day. It should be rugged enough to be interesting, because, with no trees, you would want a bit of contrast, and of course, it needs to be green. It wants to be fertile, but there must be peat to burn, and rock ledges, on which birds may nest to provide food. It should be large enough to have secret places, where a man can find privacy, and there has to be just one landing place, so that you could keep an eye on who comes and goes. You'd want your sea pretty deep offshore, so waves weren't always breaking over your craft, but you wouldn't want to be too far off-shore, because you would want to be able to row to the mainland, without spending a night at sea. You might like a bit of sandy beach, that interesting things would wash up on, and there'd be at least one protected val-ley, so the corn wouldn't always blow down. There'd be a few flagstones, ideally, with which to build your ora-tory, and beehive huts, and back dykes, to keep the cattle in. You'd keep a few black cattle, which you would bleed rather than slaughter. You'd want to keep goats, as well as sheep, because goats eat down the sor-rel on the cliffs, so the sheep are not so tempted there, and you wouldn't keep pigs, not because of the smell, but because of the way they poach pasture. While it's forever raining, as it is these days, you've got to con-serve pasture. You wouldn't fish, or not at sea, for you couldn't afford to lose men and boat.'

'You said we would *burn* the boat, Father! It's not built to last long.'

'I expect we will. I suppose we must. I'm just indulging myself here. It's been my policy, heretofore, not to ask about the island, for like a fowler blindfold on the ledge, I'm better off not knowing. But I dare say what I've described to you is a Promised Land. Am I right? Is Fairyland a Promised Land? I expect it's more of a desert.'

'It has elements of the Promised Land, but there

was barren rock, though not all barren. Fairyland was green. You see, there were two islands, Father. I ought to have mentioned that.'

'Two islands? A mirror plane. But that should come as no surprise, for I have neglected to mention the most important aspect of the perfect isle. A perfect isle is always part of a group. It must have a twin. There must be a near neighbour close by, always the hidden object of one's eye. The contemplation of wilderness is essential to human life. There could be no yardstick, apart from a ship at sea, by which to determine scale, so no one could ever be completely certain how far it was across the strait. Am I getting warm?'

'Yes Father.'

'I might have another sleep. The Lord has seen us through winter.'

Finally, the boat was built and it was time to go searching for the Land where Stories End. Despite incorporation of ribs made of the wood from the fast-growing oak, the currach was terribly ponderous and prone to capsize in any swell. It broached continually, and as none of the monks could swim, the party was soon reduced in number. Those who remained sang Songs of Praise while rowing in and out and up and down, but no sign of Fairyland could be found, within twelve kilometres of the shore. Furthermore, chants need reverberation, as provided by an oratory. Monks don't like to sing at sea.

One early summer's night there was mutiny. The saint, who always acted as sweep on the voyages, came under attack.

'This is madness!' pronounced Bran. 'We're all going to die right here! That boat is too big for six men to row. We can't keep her properly pointing at the sea. Today, we lost another colleague. What's to become of us, Father?'

'Don't blame him,' said the woodcutter. 'I'm to blame for this. I underestimated the distance of the island from the shore. I'm sorry, lads.'

'How do we find an invisible island? How do we tell where it is? Do we wait till we bump into it and sink? I'm pulling out. I've had enough.'

'Yes me too,' said the monk Darnoc. 'I'll be the next to drown!'

The woodcutter, as the biggest and strongest monk, was also the best rower, but he could never see where they going, with an oar in his hand, as he looked towards the mainland.

'I'll take an oar tomorrow,' said Finn. 'The wood-cutter can hold the sweep. Standing up and looking forward, he may be better placed to see the Land where Stories End.'

The saint had hitherto kept the monks uninformed of the island's leprechaun name, because it wasn't clear, even to fairies, whether leprechauns were fairies. If they weren't, then Jesus Christ had had nothing to say in regard of them. The saint could see, from his monks' mood, that he was losing authority over them, and having himself broken with the Pope, his powers of retaliation were reduced. So he decided he'd tell them everything that God and the woodcutter had said.

'Co-warriors,' he said, 'there are two islands, according to our recruit. One of them, which is not a Fairyland, we ought to be able to find. That will allow us to plot the position of the other, which is close by the first.'

'But we've seen no land at all!'

'True. Now God spoke to me of one island, but this man saw two, one white, the other green. Let him speak. He was guided, on his voyage, by a leprechaun.'

Every one of their sacred books had been washed overboard by now. That is why, today, no one knows what Jesus Christ said to the fairy folk.

'Cheer up lads!' said the woodcutter. 'Tomorrow, we'll show great courage. We'll head off without a thought of return and that way we'll have to succeed. The reason I know that one of those islands is not a Fairyland, is because it's covered in poos. It is white because it is a gannetry, and gannets are white and so is gannet poos. A leprechaun told me fairies don't do wees and poos so they can't be fairy gannets. Nor do males lay eggs, and I suspect there could be no hens on the Land where Stories End. Therefore, the white island I saw is not the Fairyland of Innisfinn.'

'But why are the islands not where you said?'

'I can't answer that.'

'Fair enough.'

Dawn was a fast-moving blue patch and a flesh tint under the cloud, as the currach went out, headed due west, into a short, sharp, shuddering sea. Five monks and Finn pulled at the oars while a seventh bailed. The woodcutter stood alone in the stern. They had built the boat far too large and one breaker astern would sink her.

Glancing behind him, the woodcutter kept his eyes on the hill over his own clachan. He thought, with sadness, of his wife and family. A pity things hadn't worked out. The hill, cloud-covered, grew fainter in the distance till, eventually, it disappeared.

They rowed, night and day, for several days, never once singing psalms or saying prayers, till all they could see about their boat were the fowls of the open sea: fulmars gliding beside the boat, auks with their businesslike wingbeat, shears and petrels skimming through the troughs, once in a while, a common gull.

The monks were starting to forget their beautiful plainsong chants that had to be learned by rote.

Late one day, the woodcutter shouted at the crew to lift their oars, as a wall of water, high again as the surrounding sea, bore down upon them. It started to curl and break as it bore the currach high above the surge, until, with a roar, the surge passed beneath.

In that instant, struggling to keep his boat from broaching as she surfed the glassy swell, the woodcutter saw, converging from all compass points, an infinity of gannets. And there was a blue shape in the distant mist.

When herdsmen arrived, with stone axes, they preferred to settle offshore, where wind and spray had cleared the pasture of trees. An island became, by their definition, any rock with a sheep on it, and sheep soon reduced these islands to flat mats of sea-pink and buckshorn plantain. The fertile, ungrazed island, by contrast, has fescue grass ankle-deep amid scentless mayweed, silverweed, sorrel and lovage, with its huge flowerhead wrapped in a green glans. Sea parrots (puffins) colonize these islands and their discarded breeding bills of blue, yellow and red, litter the fescue. In summer, beatles and flies abound, for a puffin will not eat a fly. Trailing their orange feet, they wheel as they return from the feeding grounds, and the turbulence from their carousels is like a helicopter's downdraught. But how can a parrot catch a second, third or fourth, sprat in its bill, while retaining the first? Both parents feed the chick, which they tend in a burrow they have commandeered, and the air above a puffinry, in summer, teems with parrots that often collide mid-air. They frequently enter the wrong burrow. Given their gruff, deep voices, the fertile, ungrazed island sounds, in summer, like fifty thousand leprechauns spying their favourite sweetmeats on a table. Over and above the growling and wolf-whistling is the maniac cackle of their predator, the greater blackbacked gull, who inverts them, while strutting the veldt with a lion's aplomb.

A puffinry of any size so undermines the soil, that

a fertile, ungrazed island eventually slides into the sea, leaving behind a perfect site for a gannetry.

The stench of ammonia became so strong, the seasick were revitalized. Gannets, or solan geese, are birds with a two-metre wingspan, and as they take to the air, they void their bellies to lighten their load. Frightened out of their limited wits by the currach's unexpected appearance, the nesting birds took off. The boat lay under their flight path, so that crew and saint were drenched with a vile-smelling, semi-molten torrent of steaming urea. The weight of this was so great as to capsize the ill-constructed craft.

'This is no Fairyland,' spluttered the woodcutter, as he resurfaced.

'Indeed no,' exclaimed the saint, 'but God has provided us meat!'

'Settle down, settle down,' grinned Bran. 'We don't meddle with these roosters.'

It wasn't clear where they might land. Solan geese will always build their nests of weeds and poos, but there wasn't much to be seen by way of vegetation, from the sea. The first hundred metres of these two-hundred-metre-high sea cliffs were bare except for sorrel, and the prevailing winds had turned them into a maze of vertical caves. Bran saw hope in the blue-black gabbro of which the island was composed, for gabbro is admired by climbers for its tacky, adhesive grip. They would be able to clamber up, but there were no convenient ledges on which to land the boat.

And Bran was right about the gannet. No fowler ventures, without fear, onto a gannetry. The gannet's bill, designed to part ocean waves at terminal velocity, is not long and thin like a seapie's bill (or a penis built by Providence to circumvent a hard plug); it is not short and hooked, like a razorbill's bill, accidental capture of which brings a lavy hunt to premature conclusion; no, it most closely resembles a weapon; something between a claymore and a dirk, shortbodied, thick at the hilt, but tapering rapidly to a point. There is no man who would not rather jump than succumb to a dozen of these. And while gannet will seldom attack a man they can see is a man, the solan geese are fowled on a moonless night.

If they could find no landing place, a crew would need to stay on the currach at all times, to keep it at sea, or else it would break up. Exhausted through ina-nition, but glad to see soil of any kind, the monks circumnavigated the desert, looking for a place to land. The woodcutter suspected this was not the desert he had previously seen, but he said nothing of this, as he also knew it would have to do. The constant capsiz-ing of the massive currach, built to his own poor design, had devastated the party of all they needed for monas-tic life.

The only place they could dare make a jump for land was a cave they found. The sea in the tunnel to this cave was green, compared with the azure of the ocean, and a couple of seals were sitting on a slimy rock by the cave entrance. A shag colony nearby betrayed its presence with a veil of poos, that looked as though someone, setting out to paint the cave, had dropped a barrel of whitewash.

Had the island been a puffinry, the high cliffs would have teemed with fulmar, each preparing to spew a flammable oil in its self-defence, as bonxies (skuas), greater blackbacked gulls and hooded crows cruised by in search of unprotected chicks. Closer to the sea, there would have been colonies of lavy. There were a few lavy, on lower ledges resonant with their loud, forced laughter, but the place was primarily a gannetry, and a fowler prefers his gannetry offshore on some uninhabited stac. He doesn't want to live on his gannetry. He'd rather live on his fulmary, as a fulmar is comparatively harmless.

'This'll do fine,' said Finn, nonetheless. 'The Lord has saved us as he saved Jonah.'

'I was a fowler before the Lord came into my life', said Bran. 'Now would you listen to me, all of you?' He showed them his ankles to prove his claim, and indeed, they were thick as thighs. 'You don't go barging onto geese rock. Geese like isolation. They always appoint a sentinel bird. You may take eggs in daylight, and if it's early in the season, they lay again, but fowling for geese is always done on a dark, moonless night. Adult birds fly off and leave the guga on the ledge, and when the guga are sufficiently hungry and thirsty, they waddle to the edge and flop off. And never again do they touch dry land until they feel the need to do the dirty thing.'

'How long do the guga stay on the ledges? I could eat a guga now.'

'Two weeks. Oh there is a feast to be had here above in late summer, lads. Guga are bigger than adult birds and their giben is better fat than butter. My family always staggered the crop, by judicious harvest of the eggs, so the guga would not all ripen at once. But if they don't all ripen at once, there are adults with them on the rock. You have to be careful. You have to find the sentinel bird before he finds you. While ever he calls "grog grog" to his sleeping colony, all is well. But if he calls "brr brr" the colony wake and fly off in alarm. I can see kittiwake, shag and lavy from here, but no fulmar at all.'

'We're not here to become fowlers, Bran,' said Finn. 'We're to be hermits! A hermit eats what God provides. He doesn't plot and scheme to eat. He may, perhaps, consume an egg. Is it late? Are the guga hatched?'

'I don't know, Father. I can't hear a thing from here. Shall we wait on the sea till dark?'

'No!' The monks who were never involved in conversation, now voiced their protest. As they were used to singing psalms, they spoke very well in unison. They wanted to eat eggs, blood, fledglings, adults, anything at all.

'If we upset them,' responded Bran, 'they'll abandon the rock. And where will we be then?'

'This is just a stopover. We'll not remain here, Bran. We're only here to find the Land where Stories End. I understand your impatience. I know you're starving to death. I realize you're thirsty and sun-burned. But this could be a home for us, until we find our green isle.'

'And while we're here,' said the woodcutter, 'we must acquire a few skills. We need to learn to eat our own poos and drink our own wees, for a start.'

'What?'

'I told you, Father! Fairies don't do wees and poos! I could safely visit the Land where Stories End and return, only because I was there too short a time to need to do a wees! And I had no bottles of beer. I have the solution to our intended residency on the green isle. In order to pass ourselves off as fairies, we eat our own poos and we drink our own wees.'

'Beware of the men who sit on the wall and who eat their own poos and who drink their own wees!' Bran was quoting from the Good Book. He was a scholar as well as a fowler.

Finn had noticed a large bird that was standing near the cave, incubating an egg.

'Bran,' he said, 'do you see that bird? That big fat bird? Can it fly?'

'That's a great lavy, Father. We don't see many of those. He'll have a pear-shaped egg beneath him, stuck to the rock with poos. Why not see if he'd give himself as meat?'

'Why, do you think he might? That would be a sign from God we are welcome here, would it not?'

'It would, Father. It would indeed.'

So they closed on the cave, then the saint hopped out on the rock and caught the great auk, and they ate and drank the bird raw, in the boat, except for the saint, who ate only the egg. Then they sat on the sea in the currach, so as not to upset the geese. Bran thought the geese were probably feeding guga, though he couldn't be sure, as you can't be sure, at first, what's going on two hundred metres above you.

All that night, the host of the air flew overhead going low by, and the raw meat of the great auk made the monks and the woodcutter violently ill.

The young monk Darnoc, an expert climber, felt he should be leader now, while Bran, an experienced fowler, had no doubt that he should be leader. The woodcutter, as the only man there who had set foot on Fairyland, felt he should be leader, while Finn, the spiritual leader, was disinclined to resign. Thus, the situation developed where half the party were giving orders that no one else obeyed, to the consternation of those monks who had no leadership pretensions. One of the party had died, after eating the liver of the great auk, and two were needed to hold the boat on the sea at any time, which left only one poor fellow to take the orders given. Were Darnoc to inform him that such and such a route were his preferred means to climb from the sea cave, Bran would be sure to veto the proposal as too disruptive from a fowling perspective. If the woodcutter offered a demonstration of how best to drink your own wees without a bottle, the saint would be sure to call for a session of prayer in the same breath. The Old Enemy, looking on, could only smile at this.

Bran felt the gannet needed time to adjust to the presence of men, so they hardly ventured from the cave, apart from one tentative expedition, which left the saint with three broken ribs. White with pain, he was rendered unable to climb or row for a while, and so they sat him at the entrance to the cave, whence he could wave encouragement. Holding the boat on the sea was an arduous task, made worse when the wind blew hard, and the men were obliged to take the boat as far from the cliff as they dared. The tides were meagre, because of the great depth of the ocean hereabout, but they saw there was a breaking surf when the wind blew from the south-west. The gales off the Edge of the World can rip out heather by the roots, but the wind here was never to the point that spray washed over the white island. Indeed, the prevailing south-westerlies should have been stronger than they were. A farmer could have grown kail, in planticrubs, above, with the prospect of a crop. More odd still, as Bran pointed out, he'd never seen a solitary gannetry. Every gannetry known to him was the northernmost stac or island in a group, for solan geese will never nest on wholly exposed rock.

Thus, there appeared to be something to the south that constituted a windbreak, and perhaps the Land where Stories End, but the cave entrance faced north-east, so they couldn't see south from where they hid.

It wasn't always blowing. The mist didn't alternate with sunlight every five minutes. The cloud wasn't always so thick and white you couldn't have read a compass. There were days when no cloud was to be seen, when there was no ripple on the sea, when the seals would loll about breathing as though breathing were the only strenuous act they knew, and Bran could hear what he thought were display dives of sickle-billed snipe, on the high moor. The monks wanted to secure the boat with a length of line, on such days, and set off up a sequence of diagonal ridges, as recommended by Darnoc. But Bran would not hear of it. He would not let them disturb the gannetry till he was persuaded the adult birds had gone. As soon as the adults abandoned the island, the gugas' necks could be safely wrung, but if the nesting grounds were invaded before those guga were ripe, that would be, in his view, a waste of resources in the short term, and possibly detrimental to future prospects of survival. In any event, if they were to be the first monks to live on a gannetry, they would need to abandon their cells and refectory during the breeding season, in order to lurk in the cave, or some such place, till the guga were ripe.

'I thought we were going to live on the Land where Stories End,' said the woodcutter, 'to which end, I've been drinking my wees and eating my poos.'

'What's it taste like?'

'Pretty bad. I can still taste that great auk. I don't know how to rid my mouth of the terrible taste of the auk. The problem is, I've always more to drink and eat each day. I can't subsist on my own wees and poos. I find I need to drink fresh water no matter how much water I make, and the more water I make myself, the more wees I must drink. I can see the time when I'm drinking wees, when not eating poos, all day.'

This was their plan: to wait till the gannet had left the ledge, abandoning their guga, to harvest the guga in safety, and to try to preserve as many guga as possible for the coming winter. They had no corn seed. It was anyway hard to see where they would grow corn, on the white island. Already they had started to gather salt, with which to preserve guga, by scraping it from the spray-drenched rocks around the cave entrance.

But the true Christian takes no thought for the morrow. He gathers his food. He doesn't hunt. He gathers, because he has no woman to gather on his behalf. The life of the hunter/gatherer well accords with the Christian spirit, which makes it all the more unlikely that Rome is the centre of the Christian world.

The hunter's bounty, in contrast, is at least given him of God. It is not sown by man's hand. And the fowl of the sea live off fish, the symbol of Christ's Love for his Church. Finn supposed a fowling monastery was a good compromise, and life did seem to be compromise, even to a Christian saint. But Finn yearned for rather less compromise, at this late stage of his life. He was weary of communal life, weary of preaching from books and singing psalms, of baking bread, of building huts, of living the plotting, scheming life of the farmer, which is what monastic life tends to become. He was hungry, after a long and devoted life as abbot and cenobite, hungry to be thought worthy, by God, to ascend to the stillness of thought. He wanted to be a hermit. He longed to sequester himself on some remote battlefield, far from other men, there to wage war against the Old Enemy free of interruptions. Seeing now the enthusiasm with which these boys collected salt, roaring with laughter that echoed through the tunnel, throwing lumps of kelp at each other, Finn felt old and weary of this life in which everything these boys did was controlled by his will, whether it be the time for work, or vigil, or prayer, or fasting. And when he thought of the Bible, though he had no Bible now, it was the words of the Preacher with the many wives that came first to his mind: 'Of making many books, there is no end; and much study is a weariness of the flesh. Childhood and youth are vanity; but if a man live many years and rejoice in them all, yet let him remember the days of darkness, for they shall be many.'

The woodcutter, too, was starting to repent his decision to become a monk. He wasn't much impressed by his fellow monks. Stripped of books, silenced of song through fear of upsetting the geese, how quickly they had lost all thought of doing God's will. They now behaved as though they considered themselves in command of their destiny. All knew there was a tall, invisible island somewhere to their south, yet never once did they pray to see it. Never once had they quizzed their Father as to whether he'd seen the white island in a vision. Nor did they ask the woodcutter if he recognized where he was, but this was perhaps as well, as he couldn't have given a confident answer. In short, though everything appeared, superficially, under control, in that no one was actually drowning or starving, the monks who remained alive had forgotten their mortality, the saint was beginning to feel he wished to be alone on the dry and dusty road (at which point, it becomes a dark and stormy one) and the woodcutter, who had sought to abandon his own dark and stormy road, was learning you can't easily jump from one road to another. Whichever road you have chosen is the road that has been chosen for you, and your destination, irrespective of your path, is the same in any event.

'Listen,' said Bran, 'do you hear that? I think the geese are taking off!'

The

LAND

where

STORIES

END

AS THEY STROLLED next day over the white island, roving from nest to dung-built nest, through the woodrush and the polypody fern in the lee of the gabbro rocks, wringing the necks of the great fat guga chicks, with their thick golden heads, they could no longer hear the calm sea two hundred metres below. As well as gannet there were birds of the upland moor on the white island – snipe, whimbrel, plover. The heather was not yet flowering and when it flowered it would have to battle the gales.

Waiting, with the neck of a guga in each hand, for the boat to reappear, the saint caught sight of a speck on the horizon to which he drew his monks' attention. The speck grew larger till all could see it was a tiny white boat, and when their own currach failed to reappear – as they learned later it had washed into the tunnel and wedged fast there among the rocks – they scrambled down Darnoc's chimney until, ten metres or so above the cobalt ocean, from the black gabbro, among the green sorrel and scurvy grass, amid the plaintive kittiwake's calling of its own name ('kittiwake, kittiwake'), the boat came close by the cliff, and they saw the boat was an egg, the half shell of an egg from some dinosaur, paddled, with an axe handle, by a boy. The sides of the shell were irregularly fractured, and the boat itself was only large enough for one.

'It's the maiden,' laughed the saint.

'Hi there,' cried Galahad, resting his makeshift oar on his knee. 'Can you hear me?'

'We can hear you,' shouted Bran, 'but won't you come up and speak to us?'

'No, I may not come ashore,' said the child, 'but am here to tell you of your good fortune. Rejoice, for the king, my father, has found the key to the door! He has released my half-sister from the tower and she and I are to journey to the Land where Stories Begin. She is to be queen of that land and I am to be king. In order to celebrate our departure, which will surely bring peace to the Promised Land, the king has made a further decree that all fairies of the fairer sex are to accompany us on our journey. So now there can be no fairy women on the Land where Stories End, and fare you well there.'

And with that, the child turned his tiny craft that

floated like a cork upon the waters, and using the axe handle for a paddle, rowed rapidly back towards the mainland.

Next day the saint could see the Land where Stories End to the south, but as the others could not see it, they kept throttling guga all day.

That night, after a feast of guga basted in its own giben, the monks fell snoring around a driftwood fire in the cave. All, that is, but the woodcutter, who couldn't sleep and wasn't feeling well.

'You can't see the island?' said the saint.

'I cannot see it, Father.'

The currach had been repaired now and if the day ahead were calm, they meant to visit the Land where Stories End.

'It is indeed a beautiful place,' said the saint, 'from what I can see. Made of a white stone, as white as this here stone is black. A white sandstone, I should say, with touches of quartz and rose highlights. Green atop, but no birds, although, of course, we are too far off to see them, at this distance. In overall shape it resembles a church tower with a steep double roof.'

'That's it! That's what I saw,' confirmed the woodcutter. He was stout and smelt bad, from eating his own poos. The saint sat as far from him, in the cave, as was not completely impolite.

'I'd like to probe your mind,' said the saint. 'What did the leprechaun say? What exactly did he say to you?

It's important you remember.'

The woodcutter thought hard. He had spoken so frequently with leprechauns. But with no beer to drink, his memory was working well.

'He said it was bound to appear but not to me, Father, and the truth of that is apparent, in that you can see the island which I cannot. Another thing, he said I would have to go there in order to be married. Well, as you know, that cannot be, there being no fairy women there, or females of any kind.'

'Which is why the Lord God wants me to build a monastery. Would you like to be married tomorrow, friend?'

The woodcutter thought harder.

'I always wanted to be married,' he conceded, 'but have given up the notion that marriage brings happiness, having had such bad luck with women.'

'The question is, do you *want* to be married? That's the question. That's the only question now.'

'I guess so.'

'Okay. Get in the boat.'

'What about the lads, Father? Who's going to row the boat?'

'We'll do the rowing ourselves. We don't want the lads along. There'll be no sweep for us, friend. The sea is calm.'

'Let me have the one last wees and poos before we leave.'

It was to be his last wees and his last poos. He let

the sea wash away what he produced. He didn't try to eat or drink it, thank the Lord. Then he grabbed the boat, and with effort the saint and himself pulled the boat out of the tunnel, then jumped in, and off they went towards the south, over a calm sea.

The saint could see the island but when he tried to step ashore, it wasn't there to him, and the woodcutter had to pull him from the water, half-drowned. By the same token, the woodcutter couldn't see the island, but he stepped upon it with ease, so the two of them made their way, gingerly and stealthily, the woodcutter guided by the saint, the saint riding on the woodcutter's back, over the glistening sandstone, which the woodcutter realized, from the saint's description, was indeed the Land where Stories End, but with no steps yet cut in the rock and no beehive huts and no oratory.

'Do you see any birds?' asked the woodcutter. 'Is there fowl about the place?'

'No hens, so there could be no nests and no eggs and no chicks. There is nothing to eat here.'

'Flowers?'

'Not a one. No flowers are to be seen. There are no females here, to lead men astray. Why, this is the perfect place for meditation! Do you still want to be married, friend?'

'I suppose so.'

'Then say it in a louder voice. Go on! Say it so loud the fairies hear! I sense the presence of male fairies. There are fairies about.'

All that day they explored the island, the saint describing what he saw to the woodcutter, and the woodcutter feeling more and more certain he wanted to be married, if he could be married here. This was the most beautiful place ever he had seen, if only he could see it. Sharp-eyed Bran, who had climbed to the highest peak on the white island, saw two male figures, one atop the other, roaming around in the sky above the sea. Next day, when the other monks came up to share the view with him, they were amazed to see the Land where Stories End to their south, with sunlight roving through the clouds illuminating hills of a tropical green. It had formed overnight. They couldn't wait to get across to visit, but as they had no currach, the saint having taken the boat, instead they kept up with the guga harvest, eating those birds they couldn't salt down, but now chanting psalms as they worked and staring at the Land where Stories End. It wouldn't be so bad a place to live, with this Promised Land gannetry close by.

After a few more days the weather turned a little and Finn came rowing back alone. Behind him, as he laboriously rowed, the fulmar were flocking to the Land where Stories End. Fulmar, the plankton-eating paragon of North Atlantic seafowl, is the fowler's preferred fowl, being the size and colour of a stout common gull, with salient tube nostrils and very easily seized. It never lays again or returns to its nest on the high ledge when disturbed, so a fulmary must be carefully managed. The fulmar produces eggs, meat, a flammable oil and an insect-repellant feather.

'Where is the woodcutter, Father?'

The saint smiled. 'I left him where he lay, lads. He fell down to be married. I officiated at his wedding, on the rocks at the foot of the cliff. It was a beautiful ceremony. Now we must leave before the weather worsens. This is no place for us to live, now the green island is manifest. Load the guga aboard the currach.'

'But what about the fairies, Father? How do they feel about us moving in? Isn't Jesus telling us that only fairy men can live in Fairyland?'

'We came to an agreement between us, the chief of the fairies and myself. He says we can remain on the Land where Stories End, provided we produce a minimum of wees and poos. If we produce more than humanly possible, we shall have to move off. We may sleep, provided we sleep no more than two hours a day, and if we dream of mortal or fairy women, we shall have to move off. Frankly, I think those fairies will leave before we do. I think that island must eventually become our property, for how can lonely fairy men endure a fulmar hen? As soon as the fairy chief said I can remain to build my hermitage, the island became substantial and the fulmars flocked to the ledges to provide us with all we shall need. See them, Bran?'

'I see them, Father. And a beautiful sight they make, for fulmar is the finest fowl.'

'They are a sign the Land where Stories End has

become a Christian land. It is now part way between a Fairyland and the Promised Land.'

So the monks filled the currach with fresh guga and rowed across the strait to the Land where Stories End, which became known, after the fairies left, as Innisfinn. And the monks and their successors built a village of six beehive huts and an oratory, to be their hermitage, and carved a stairway up to it out of the sandstone. And they lived by fowling, all but their founder-saint, who ate only what fell into his mouth and hands, from the talons and beaks of skuas and hooded crows and greater blackbacked gulls. And they prayed rather than slept, for fear of dreaming of fairy women, and produced as little wees and poos as was possible, in the beginning.

And if you ask who the woodcutter married, why, he married the Queen of Heaven. He married the Virgin Mary. He married that woman suggested to him by all the women he had ever loved. He married his own pure soul.

Servus Mariae numquam peribit.